THE ANTI-RELATIONSHIP YEAR

KATIE WISMER

ALSO BY KATIE WISMER

The Anti-Virginity Pact

Poems for the End of the World

The Sweetest Kind of Poison

This book contains material that may be triggering for some readers. Reader discretion is advised. For a complete list of trigger warnings, please visit katiewismer.com/trigger-warnings

INTRODUCTION

To be the first to know about new releases, giveaways,
exclusive content, and more, make sure to sign up for my
newsletter:
www.katiewismer.com

Playlist available on Spotify:
shorturl.at/vzSZ4

❧ 1 ❧

FRESHMAN YEAR - AUGUST

JOHANNA PALMER STARTED THE NIGHT IN THE LAP OF A guy she didn't know. Despite the curled lip on the Uber driver's face as the eight of them had piled into a hatchback meant for five, the kid just drummed his fingers against the steering wheel as he waited for their group to situate themselves.

Three of the four boys slid into the back seat, and the last one crouched in the trunk, leaving the four girls to fill the remaining spaces. Each chose a lap of one of the guys in the back—which was how Jo ended up with her entire right side plastered to the car door and the heat of a stranger's body pressing into her bare legs. Somehow her new roommate, Kayleigh, had scored the only seat with any semblance of personal space in the front.

The bar wasn't far, and Jo could already feel the vodka from the pregame warming her blood and loosening her limbs. But that didn't stop the nervous sweat from appearing on her palms. She'd had the fake ID since high school, but this would be her first time trying it in Oregon. Getting her card confiscated would really put a damper on her first college night out. Not that she needed more to drink—she'd panic-chugged the entire pregame—but she had no idea how to get home if they turned her away. She hadn't even memorized her new address yet.

The car jostled violently as it hit a pothole. Jo braced her hands against the roof, holding on for dear life, as the two girls next to her let out high-pitched, drunken squeals. Jo already couldn't remember their names, which probably wasn't a good sign, seeing as she'd be living with them for the next year. She'd met Kayleigh on the college's Facebook group, and when they'd managed to land a spot in one of the nicer dorms, they'd automatically been paired with two other girls for a suite.

Their rooms were pretty standard as far as dorms went —wooden furniture that looked like it belonged in a prison and a single window on the far wall—but it connected to another double, and the four of them got to share a bathroom instead of having one for the entire hall.

As far as random pairings went, it definitely could've been worse. But since the other two girls had been friends since high school, they hadn't bothered to socialize with Jo and Kayleigh much so far.

The boys lived across the hall, also all roommates, and had been the only ones on the floor to accept Kayleigh's invitation for an impromptu night out. Jo wasn't sure if it was because the rest of their hall mates weren't partiers, or because it was a Tuesday and they all had their first day of classes tomorrow morning.

The car jostled again, and this time, the boy beneath Jo grabbed her hips to steady her. His hands felt gigantic against her small frame. The heat of his palms burned against the sliver of skin exposed between her skirt and top. He released her immediately and muttered a soft "sorry" under his breath.

She could barely hear him over the rap song vibrating the car. She twisted her neck to try to get a look at him, but it was dark, and the linebacker-esque guy next to him monopolized the majority of her view. She couldn't remember any of the boys' names, either.

At least she remembered Kayleigh's—unless she'd just been calling her the wrong name all night and no one had bothered to correct her.

God, she wished Meredith were here. That friendship was so effortless, Jo never had to give anything a second thought. She supposed that was a byproduct of knowing someone since they were in diapers. But Mare was down in California now, probably also awkwardly bumping elbows with strangers with the hopes of it becoming something more. High school was over, and clinging to old habits and friends wasn't going to do her any favors.

Johanna tugged on her skirt, trying to keep it from riding up her thighs as the car bounced along. *Ugh, how mortifying.* She was totally going to flash this guy when it was time to climb out of the car. So much for first impressions.

The Uber pulled up to the corner outside the bar,

where a line of people was already stretched around the side of the building. Johanna's gaze locked on the boulder of a man checking IDs at the door, and a flush of nerves traveled down her spine. She quickly scurried out of the car as gracefully as she could manage and craned her neck back to take in the neon sign above them.

UNITED FATES
AUGUST 26 9:00 PM

The guy she'd squished the entire ride climbed out next. His body unfolded like some kind of never-ending Slinky. He had to be a least a full foot taller than she was, but not much heavier. Wavy brown hair fell into his eyes as he shoved his hands in his pockets and stepped up onto the sidewalk beside her. The other girls squealed and laughed as they climbed out, clutching hands and holding one another up. They weren't nearly that drunk yet, but the routine was clearly having its intended effect.

"Wait for *me*," the dark-skinned girl drawled as she checked her reflection in the car window and fluffed up her curly, black hair. Her southern accent was somehow even more pronounced now than when she was sober. The taller of the two boys grinned and eagerly offered his hand. His friend looped his arm around the little blonde girl's waist.

Johanna cast another uneasy glance at the bouncer. She was no expert, but there was no way making a scene before they even made it to the front of the line would work in their favor.

She eyed her lanky companion, desperately searching

her memory for his name. It was something odd, more of a last name. "You're...Miller, right?" Jo asked, wincing.

He nodded, seemingly oblivious to her struggle. "You're Johanna."

"Just Jo."

"All right, Just Jo. I say we ditch the lunatics and get in line." He jabbed his thumb at the two girls piggybacking on the other guys while the boy in the trunk, not to be forgotten, beat frantically on the window.

Jo raised her eyebrows. "No loyalty to your friends?"

He shrugged, but reached over and popped the trunk to let the last guy out. "I actually don't know any of them. I just let the school randomly assign me to a room."

"Really? That seems risky. What if you're, like, zero percent compatible?"

"Can we go inside now?" Kayleigh fell into step beside them, adjusting her jean skirt. "And maybe pretend that we're *not* with them," she added under her breath.

Jo smirked and hooked her arm through Kayleigh's without thinking about it—it was just something she'd always done with her best friend from home. If Kayleigh was taken aback, she didn't show it. Jo held out her other arm. "Oh, come on, Miller," she said. "Don't feel left out."

To her surprise, he grinned—both cheeks dimpling as he did—and took it.

"THEY'RE SENIORS AT PORTLAND STATE," KAYLEIGH hissed under her breath as the bouncer glanced at their

IDs and ushered them inside. Miller wiggled his eyebrows as the three of them hurried through the doors. The bar was lively, but not as crowded as Jo had expected. The stage was just a small platform in the back corner with a few lights pointed in its direction. Wires and musical instruments were strewn about, but none of the band members had surfaced yet.

"I've never heard of them," Jo admitted.

"They're about to make it big," Kayleigh insisted, raising onto her tiptoes to get a look at the line out the windows. "I can't see Addie or Liv anymore." She turned to Miller. "What are your roommates' names again?"

Miller frowned and shrugged.

Jo stifled a snort. At least it wasn't just her.

"You don't know any of their names?" Kayleigh demanded.

Miller narrowed his eyes, considering this. "Pretty sure one of them is Alan—big guy with the goofy hair? And one of them might be Gatsby. Or maybe he just likes *The Great Gatsby*..." He shook his head. "Nah, he doesn't seem like the kind to read. I think it's his name."

Kayleigh threw her hands up, her gaze now moving on to survey the rest of the crowd—a few people were wearing T-shirts with the name *UNITED FATES* scrawled across the front, but not many. She jutted her chin toward the bar and elbowed Jo in the ribs. "You should get the drinks. You look the most twenty-one of the three of us."

Jo shot an uneasy glance toward the bar and adjusted the straps of her tank top. She already had the wristband from the front door. The hard part was over. She forced a

THE ANTI-RELATIONSHIP YEAR

smile and flipped her hair over her shoulders. She'd curled it tonight, and the tinted lights overhead were making it look more wine-colored than its usual copper shade. "I'll be right back."

The bartender did a quick once-over as she approached. "What can I get you?" His hair was nearly as red as Johanna's was, complete with a matching mustache. He also looked to be barely twenty-one himself.

"Three beers." Her gaze swept the bar, and she pointed to a fish-shaped tap handle. "That one." She had no idea if *that one* was any good, but the bartender turned away wordlessly and grabbed three glasses.

"Those all for you?"

A man slid into the chair on Johanna's left. The first thing she noticed was the tattoos. He braced an arm on the bar, revealing a sleeve all the way from his wrist to his shoulder beneath his white T-shirt. All of the images and words blurred seamlessly together, the black ink stark against his pale skin. A silver coin on a long chain dangled from his neck as he leaned forward.

The second thing she noticed was how inky and gelled his hair was, styled to stand up just-so in the front. He must have spent at least half as long as she had in front of the mirror tonight.

The final thing she noticed was the way his eyes lingered on her body. He found her face eventually, but it was a steep climb to get there. He started at her legs, then gradually made it to her hips, her waist, her chest, and then, finally, her eyes. He wasn't even being subtle about it. He *wanted* her to see him looking at her.

From what she could tell, he had a nice body, too. But she definitely wasn't about to give him the satisfaction of watching *her* check *him* out.

"I don't have NPS tattooed on my lip for nothing," she said as the bartender returned and slid the beers across the counter to her.

"NPS?" asked the mystery guy.

She quirked an eyebrow at him over her shoulder. "No pussy shit."

His entire face lit up around his laugh as he tossed a wad of cash toward the bartender. "They're on me."

"That doesn't mean I'm going to share them with you," she said as she juggled the three glasses against her chest. The condensation was cold against her skin, and a bead of water rolled down her cleavage as she stood and turned to go.

The man stood too, his body dangerously close to hers, and blocked her exit. He was taller, but not overwhelmingly so. Maybe four inches. His shoulders were broader than she'd first realized, though, and shit, he smelled good.

Slowly, she raised her eyes to meet his in what she hoped was a defiant look.

"If we don't bore you too much, maybe I'll see you after the show."

She blinked, processing his words. "You're in the band," she concluded.

He inclined his head toward her. "Smart, too."

A flash of movement caught the corner of her vision, and she glanced up to see Kayleigh waving at her from the center of the crowd. It was noticeably thicker than when she'd gone to the bar. Jo nodded her head to the side. "I should get back to my friends."

The man stepped back and gestured for her to pass. She was barely two paces away when he called after her, "Hey! Do you really have that tattoo?"

She glanced at him over her shoulder, this time letting her eyes travel the length of him. She smiled a bit and said, "I guess you'll never know."

People were crowding around the stage by the time Johanna reached the others, now with Liv, Addie, and the other three boys in tow. Jo could feel the man's eyes on her as she walked away, and she'd be lying if she said she hadn't purposefully overexaggerated the sway of her hips as she moved.

The extra beers had barely left her hands before Kayleigh squealed, "Do you have any idea who you were just talking to?"

Jo glanced over her shoulder again, but the guy from the bar was gone. When she turned back around, Kayleigh was beaming. She opened her mouth to say more, but then the overhead lights dimmed, and the room erupted in shouts and applause as the band crowded onto the small stage. The drummer and guitar player looked like sisters, both donning long, brown hair and deeply tanned skin.

But it was the lead singer Johanna couldn't look away from.

There was something different about his presence now that he was on stage. He stood tall, shoulders thrown back, but everything about him radiated ease. His features looked almost contemplative as he pulled the microphone from its stand and scanned the crowd. The moment his gaze landed on Jo, heat burned from the roots of her hair to the tips of her toes. His grin widened at the sight of her, and to her horror, he pointed at her, causing dozens of heads to turn in her direction.

"This first song is for the girl whose name I *will* get out of her before the end of the night."

HALF OF THE CROWD DISAPPEARED BEFORE THE END OF the set, but the half that remained was eating up every second of it. The music was a little too punk for Johanna's taste, but she had to admit, the man knew how to work a crowd. Every few minutes, his eyes would find her again, and it momentarily pinned her to the spot. His skin glowed beneath the spotlights, and he had the type of contagious energy that immediately electrified the rest of the room. Even the people who didn't know the lyrics were bouncing around, sweating and screaming and grinding against one another—Kayleigh being one of them. Despite herself, Jo found herself bobbing to the beat and letting Kayleigh rope her into her dancing. Miller mainly just stood there, but at least he was smiling.

Once the band finished their final song and the spotlights flickered off, the majority of the members headed for the bar, groups of fans trailing after them. Johanna's mystery man, however, was nowhere to be seen.

Addie and Liv had already dipped out halfway through the set with the other boys, taking an Uber back to campus to catch some house party near their dorm. Johanna did another quick scan of the crowd.

"Should I order an Uber?" Miller suggested.

"No," Kayleigh whined and stuck her lower lip out. She slung her arm over Jo's shoulders, leaning more weight onto Jo than she'd expected, and they both stumbled to the side. "Not until Jo gives that guy her number."

"I'm not giving anyone my number," said Jo as she clung to Kayleigh's arm, trying to keep them both upright.

"Well that's a shame."

She jumped at the deep voice behind her and whipped around.

The lead singer ran a hand through his hair, pushing it back from his face, his white T-shirt now clinging to his chest with sweat. "I don't believe I had the chance to introduce myself before. I'm Greyson, but you can call me Grey."

"Her name's Johanna!" Kayleigh nearly cried out. "But she goes by Jo."

Jo shot her a disbelieving look. *Traitor.*

"Johanna." Grey smiled as he said it, like he liked the way her name tasted in his mouth. "Let me buy you a drink."

"We were just leaving," said Jo.

He was beautiful—she wasn't oblivious. But he also looked like trouble, something Johanna was desperately trying to avoid. College was her fresh start. She wasn't going to ruin that the very first week just because some guy in a band looked good in leather pants and had long eyelashes.

"*Well*," said Kayleigh. "There's a wait for an Uber anyway..."

Grey stepped forward, close enough that the earthy smell of him flooded her senses. He lifted a lock of her hair and twisted the curl around his fingers. She forced herself to keep a neutral expression, but her breath caught in her throat. "So what'll it be, Johanna?" he murmured. "One beer?"

Jo pursed her lips and cast her gaze toward the long line of people waiting for a car on the sidewalk. "I'm going to go wait at that table over there." She pointed to one of the bar tables near the door. "And if you can get one before the Uber gets here, then fine."

Grey grinned, accepting the challenge, and wove back through the crowd toward the bar, shrugging off girls who threw their hands at him as he went. Kayleigh opened her mouth, but Jo held up a finger to stop her.

"Don't. Say. Anything."

"I'll be by the bar," Miller announced, and when Kayleigh hesitated by Jo's side, he reached over, hooked his arm through Kayleigh's elbow, and hauled her along with him. Jo sighed, ventured over toward the windows, and slid into one of the stools. The crowd started to thin as people filtered out the door, a few pausing just outside to smoke.

"Peace offering."

Grey slid a beer across the table to Jo. The chatter of the bar and clamoring of equipment as the rest of the band packed up faded to the background as he came into focus. He braced his forearms on the narrow table and leaned forward, leaving barely a foot of space between their faces.

He had blue eyes, Johanna realized. A detail she hadn't noticed before.

She sipped the beer and raised her eyebrows.

"You don't like it," said Grey.

Jo took another sip and tilted her head to the side, considering. She wasn't a fan of beer in general, but this one had a sort of citrusy aftertaste. She couldn't decide how she felt about it. "It's not bad."

His lips turned up. "You seem very hard to please."

"Maybe you're just not used to being around people who have standards."

He leaned back in his chair, his laugh crinkling the corners of his eyes. "I like you, Johanna."

She set the beer back down. "You don't know me."

He raised his palms, smile still entirely intact. "Not from lack of trying."

Jo spotted Miller out of the corner of her eye. He was hesitating by the bar, sipping his new beer, eyes flicking from Kayleigh talking beside him to Jo's table every few seconds.

She turned back to Grey, and his gaze bored into hers. It felt like a challenge. But there was so much intensity in his eyes, so much heat, that Johanna's cheeks warmed despite herself, and she was the first to lower her gaze. She spun the beer between her palms, focusing on the cold glass against her skin.

"Let me take you out sometime," he said. "Somewhere without your friend staring at us from the bar. Somewhere you'll actually let me get to know you."

Against her better judgement, she looked up. His wide,

blue eyes searched hers. A flash of heat shot through her chest. She should've said no. God, she knew she *needed* to say no. But somehow, she found herself straightening in her chair and forcing a coy smile onto her face. "Fine. But you only get one hour."

This time when he leaned in close, he wasn't smiling. Something like wicked amusement danced in his eyes as he whispered, "Baby, one hour is all I need."

❧ 2 ❧

SENIOR YEAR - MARCH

THE LAST LIGHT IN THE HALL FLICKERED OUT, JOLTING JO out of her trance. She leaned back in her chair and rubbed her eyes; Photoshop burned in the backs of her eyelids. There was something not quite right. She blew the air out of her cheeks and leaned forward again to sift through the layers one last time. She'd been tinkering with the same photo for nearly an hour now, but it still wasn't perfect. And it was the opening image for her portfolio, so it needed to be.

She squinted a single eye shut and tilted her head to the side. Maybe she'd been wasting her time. Maybe she should've just left the photo in black and white like she'd originally planned—

"You know, if I were a murderer, you would totally be dead by now."

Jo jumped and spun her chair around. Miller stood a few paces behind her in sweaty workout clothes, a brown paper bag in hand. He glanced around the empty computer lab—the only light coming from Jo's screen and the emergency fixture above the door—then looked back to her.

"How long have you been standing there?" she demanded.

He stared at her blankly. "Several minutes."

"Miller!"

He held up his hands. "I said your name like three times."

"Oh." She rubbed her eyes again. "Sorry. I've just been freaking out trying to get my portfolio perfect before the final showcase."

He braced his arms on the desk around her and leaned down to inspect the screen. The shot she'd been working on was a close-up profile of a girl from her advanced photography workshop. Jo had slicked back her hair to show off her bone structure and added a lacy shadow over half of her face.

Miller made a low *hmm* noise in the back of his throat and straightened. "Looks pretty perfect to me, like always."

Jo's eyes shot to the bag he'd set on the desk. "What's in there?"

"Well, I thought I might find you in here, and I also figured you forgot to eat dinner again, so I swung by the dining hall after class."

"Dinner?" She pulled out her phone, a small jolt going through her chest at the sight of 10:02 p.m.—though she supposed she should've assumed as much from Miller's appearance. His boxing class didn't let out until 9:30. A

slew of texts littered her screen, all from Jordan, all deriva-
tives of *we still on for tonight?* "Shit," she muttered.

Miller quirked an eyebrow and glanced sideways at her
phone. "Please tell me that isn't Teacher's Pet."

Jo smiled innocently and powered down the computer.

Miller scoffed. "I thought you ended things with him
weeks ago."

Jo shrugged and slung her backpack over her shoulder.
"It's a small school, and these are desperate times." She
leaned forward to peek in the bag, but he snatched it out
of reach.

"Absolutely not. I am not rewarding poor decisions
with pasta."

She batted her eyelashes. "You'd rather I starve?"

He narrowed his eyes. "Fuck." He tossed the bag at her.
"Just let it be known that I voiced my disapproval."

She nodded seriously, already fishing the plastic fork
out of the bag. "Duly noted."

"And please," he added as they slipped into the dark
hallway. "For the love of God, never share any details
with me."

THE MAJORITY OF THE ATTRACTION WITH JORDAN LAID
in the convenience. He had an apartment in the same
building as Jo and Miller, though his was several floors
higher up. And as far as college boy apartments went, it
wasn't...horrible. Jo had certainly been in worse. If nothing
else, he had the view going for him. Three tall windows

covered the back wall and looked out toward the mountains. The rest of the apartment was minimally furnished—a leather couch from Goodwill in the corner, a flat screen TV on the wall, a mattress on the floor. At least he put sheets on the bed before Jo showed up.

He had a bottle of wine waiting on the kitchen island, and Jo eagerly accepted a glass, her eyes drifting to whatever medical drama was playing on the TV. Whether he was watching it for himself or he put it on because he thought she'd like it—she didn't ask.

He rolled up the sleeves of his gray hoodie and leaned against the counter, twisting the wine glass between his hands. His round glasses were noticeably absent tonight, his curly blonde hair pushed back from his face. Light stubble lined his jaw, more than usual. He opened his mouth like he was going to say something, but quickly closed it.

Jo raised an eyebrow. "What?"

He shook his head, smiling a little. "I was going to ask how your paper for Wells' class was going, but thought better of it."

Her eyebrow lifted another inch, and she skimmed her fingertips across the counter as she paced toward him, stopping only once their bodies were inches apart. Jordan stood up a little taller.

"Thought better of it because you assume it's going poorly?"

Truthfully, she hadn't even started it yet—hadn't worked on anything but her portfolio in nearly a week. It would probably take an all-nighter at this point, but she'd get it done.

His eyes flicked down to her mouth. "Thought better of it because I assumed you didn't want to talk about class tonight. Unless you came here for tutoring, because then I think we really got our wires crossed."

"We've talked about you talking less, right?" She grabbed the back of his head, her fingers knotting in his hair. "I thought we talked about this." A single corner of her mouth curled as she said it, and she leaned forward until their lips were close enough to brush, but not quite. She was only half kidding. She'd spent the entire elevator ride up here brainstorming ways to occupy him so he wouldn't have the chance to ask *how's that?* every five seconds.

He nodded quickly. "Yep. Shutting up now."

At least this time when they kissed, there was less tongue than usual—a gradual buildup instead of an outright attack. There was only so much Jo could do, but at least he was slightly trainable. His hands slid down the backs of her legs, cupped her thighs, and hoisted her into his arms. She locked her legs around his waist as he carried her toward his room, his lips never breaking from hers. The mattress slid along the wood floor as they collapsed on top of it. Every time he opened his mouth and looked like he was going to talk, she reached up and pulled him in for another kiss. His stubble scraped along her skin as his lips trailed down her neck.

And then, unfortunately, the tongue reappeared full force. He licked from her collarbone to just below her ear and leaned over to do the same on the other side. Jo squeezed her eyes shut, but the damage was done. Whatever mood she'd managed to muster for herself was gone.

"Jordan." She pushed herself up on her elbows, and he pulled back, his eyes half closed. She trailed her hands down his arms braced on either side of her, fingers tracing over the cords of muscle and veins standing out in his forearms. She forced herself to pause and consider her words.

"It was the tongue thing, wasn't it?" he asked.

She grimaced.

"Can we try one more time?" He leaned forward, his lips brushing her ear as he whispered, "I won't disappoint, I promise."

Jo very much doubted that, but forced a smile onto her face and nodded.

JORDAN ALWAYS FELL ASLEEP SHORTLY AFTER, HIS SNORES filling the apartment around them. Jo stared at the traces of moonlight on the ceiling for a moment, before tilting her head to look at him. He was passed out on his back, his lips slightly parted, one arm thrown over his head. His chest rose and fell in a slow rhythm. His other arm lay between them, slightly extended toward her side of the bed like he was reaching for her.

It should've been sweet. It should've been everything she wanted, and maybe four years ago, it would've been. But looking at Jordan's peaceful profile, no matter how hard she tried, it made her feel absolutely nothing at all. And maybe that was the point.

She gently lifted the sheets and slid from the bed, squinting for her clothes in the dim light.

"Hey." The bed shifted beneath her, and Jordan's fingers brushed against her arm. "You leaving?"

Finding her sweatshirt on the floor beside the mattress, she grabbed it and yanked it back over her head. "Yeah, sorry if I woke you."

The sheets rustled and his breath tickled the back of her neck as he came up to rest his chin on her shoulder. "You could stay, if you wanted." His arms curled around her stomach and pulled her back against his chest. "I was thinking maybe we could do that more. Maybe hang out... other times."

Jo sighed and closed her eyes. She'd really been hoping it wasn't going to come to this. "I don't think that's a good idea, Jordan. I should get home." She untangled herself from him and stood, searching the ground for her leggings.

He watched her from the edge of the mattress and ran a hand through his hair. "I like you, Jo. More than just four-a.m.-phone-calls like you."

She jumped as she shimmied into her leggings and blew the hair out of her eyes. "Look, Jordan, it's not that I don't like you. We've had fun. I'm just not looking for anything more than that. I'm not doing relationships right now. Not with you—not with anyone."

He locked his hands together in front of him, looked at the floor, and nodded slowly. It was probably one of the most pitiful things Jo had ever seen.

The smart thing to do would be to keep walking without another word. It was the coddled feelings that got them here in the first place. But still, seeing him like that, it reminded her of a version of herself she didn't like to think about anymore.

She knelt down in front of him and placed her hands on his shoulders, shaking him until he finally looked at her. He pressed his lips together in a sad excuse for a smile. "Got it."

"I'll see you around, Jordan." Then she leaned forward, kissed him lightly on the cheek, and left.

FRESHMAN YEAR - AUGUST

KAYLEIGH ROSE ONTO HER TIPTOES AS SHE STRUNG THE hot pink sheet across the room, tucking it between the lofted beds. A sea of blankets and pillows were already situated on the floor between them, the fort already fully stocked with three boxes of Lime-a-ritas and a family-sized bag of potato chips.

"Don't knock the whole thing down!" Addie scolded as Liv climbed on Kayleigh's desk to secure the other sheet across the back, this one a far less assaulting shade of lavender. Liv rolled her eyes as she hopped back down, her bunny slippers making a soft *thud* against the floor. Her curly black hair was pulled back in two braids and whipped around her shoulders as she collapsed onto the floor and eagerly grabbed a drink from the middle.

Jo tucked herself into the corner beside her bed and cracked open a can, watching as Kayleigh finished constructing their masterpiece. She'd brought down the string lights that usually hung above her bed and wound them around on the floor. They glowed against the bright sheets and cast a pink tint to everyone's faces.

"Perfect!" Kayleigh ducked inside and plopped down across from Jo, her oversized T-shirt billowing out around her like a tent.

The entire room hummed with giddy energy as Liv thrust her Lime-a-rita into the middle of their circle. "I want to go first!" she announced. "Never have I ever..." She tilted her head to the side as she considered her next words, her grin slowly twisting into something mischievous. "Had sex with another woman."

"Oh, real nice." Addie rolled her eyes and threw back a sip of her drink.

Jo watched with wide eyes as Kayleigh also tipped her can back. When she caught Jo looking, Kayleigh shrugged. "Senior beach week."

"My turn!" Addie swiveled her head to raise her eyebrows at Liv. "Never have I ever done *cocaine*."

"I'm not ashamed of that," Liv said matter-of-factly and took a long swig from her drink.

"Are the two of you just going to keep targeting each other all night?" Kayleigh demanded.

"By all means," said Addie. "Give us a good one."

Kayleigh shifted and crossed her legs, balancing her drink on her knee. "Never have I ever..." She narrowed her eyes a bit. "Gotten so drunk I've thrown up."

Jo, Addie, and Liv all raised their cups and laughed.

"Cheers, ladies!" Liv sang, clanking her can against the others before eagerly gulping down another mouthful.

When she was done, she crushed the can in her fist and tossed it vaguely in the direction of the trash can by the door. Her gaze shot from Addie's face to the drink in her hand. "Looks like you're already behind."

"Maybe I'm just pacing myself," said Addie.

Kayleigh nudged Jo with her knee. "Your turn."

All three girls turned to her expectantly. Jo drummed her nails on her can, her mind suddenly blank. She didn't have anything even remotely in the same league as the rest of them.

"Come on!" said Liv. "What's the first thing that pops into your head?"

An image from senior year flashed into Jo's mind—the one moment she'd been pointedly trying *not* to think about ever since it happened. But without it, her history was a slew of near misses and false starts—nothing worth *oohing* and *ahhing* over. Nothing that was really that interesting at all.

Addie leaned over and whispered something in Liv's ear. They exchanged a knowing glance, and Liv covered her mouth with her hand to hide her giggle.

It was a look Jo was all too familiar with—the quick glances, the hushed voices that were oftentimes *just* loud enough to hear, and not by accident. To be honest, Addie and Liv weren't even that good at it. The real skill came in the subtlety. The voices that crawled over your skin. The biting comments with just enough truth to them to burrow in. If Addie and Liv thought this little routine was having any effect, they were going to be sorely disappointed.

Jo pressed her lips together and tightened her fist

around her drink. "Never have I ever kissed a teacher."

Then she raised the can and drank.

The room erupted in squeals and gasps.

"What!" said Addie.

"Details!" added Liv.

Kayleigh grabbed Jo's arm and gave it a little shake. "Oh my God, *pause*. We need the full story on this one."

Honestly, just thinking about it made Jo feel like she was about to throw up, but she forced a sly smile onto her face and gave an overexaggerated shrug. "I never kiss and tell."

"Bullshit!" cried Addie.

Before the other girls could chime in their objections, there was a faint knock on the door. They all froze and exchanged wide-eyed glances. Jo instinctively hid her drink behind her back.

"RA?" mouthed Kayleigh.

Another knock. "It's Miller!"

"Oh!" Liv jumped up and threw the door open. Miller waved awkwardly from the hall in black sweatpants and a gray hoodie, his dark hair curling into his eyes.

"Girls only!" Kayleigh called.

"Oh, let him in," said Liv.

"Yeah, Miller's not, like, a real boy anyway." Addie grabbed his sleeve and pulled him inside, kicking the door shut behind him.

He fell into the spot beside Jo, his knee resting against hers. She grabbed a drink from the middle and handed it to him. "So are you, like, Pinocchio now?"

He smirked and bumped her shoulder with his. "*I'm a*

real boy!'"

"We're playing *Never Have I Ever,*" said Kayleigh. "And Jo was just about to tell us—"

"It's Miller's turn now," said Jo.

Miller's gaze ping-ponged between the two of them. "I have no idea what that means."

"You say something you've never done," Jo explained. "And if anyone else *has* done it, they have to drink."

"Like Liv's snorted cocaine," said Addie. "And Jo's made out with her teacher."

"I never said *made out*—"

Kayleigh grabbed the chip bag from the center of the circle and tore it open. "Give us a good one, Miller."

He raised his hands and shook his head helplessly. "I don't—I —"

Liv waved her hands impatiently. "He just joined. We'll go around the circle again so he can see some more examples. So it's Addie's turn again."

Addie grinned, tossed aside her empty can, and grabbed another from the box in the middle. She hummed as she tapped her nails against the top. "Oh! I have a good one. Never have I ever gone to college as a *virgin.*" She wiggled her eyebrows and scanned the circle with narrowed eyes.

Fuck. Jo sighed and took a sip. Her stomach clenched as none of the other girls drank, and a small, satisfied smirk rose to Liv's lips. But then she realized Miller was doing the same beside her.

"We have *two* virgins in here!" Liv leaned forward and pointed a finger at Miller. "You? No offense, but expected. But *you?*" She swiveled to Jo. "I'm surprised."

Jo straightened a bit, refusing to crumble under her gaze.

"Not, like, in a bad way," Kayleigh jumped in.

"No," agreed Addie.

"Why haven't you?" Liv asked, now moving onto her third drink. Between her and Addie, they were already down one box, and they'd only started drinking half an hour ago. Judging by Liv's slurring words, she and Addie may have started before they'd gotten here.

Addie scrunched up her face. "Is it a Jesus thing?" She turned to Miller. "Jesus thing?"

"Not a Jesus thing," said Miller.

"Oh leave them alone." Kayleigh hopped up to toss her can in the trash and paused to collect Addie and Liv's that were scattered along the ground. "I think it's sweet."

"Well Jo has that band guy now," said Liv. "So it probably won't be for much longer."

Jo rolled her eyes. "I don't *have* anyone. I agreed to one date."

Addie and Liv smirked at each other.

"He's totally going to try to get in your pants," said Liv.

"Totally," agreed Addie.

"Wait." Liv leaned forward. "Are you like a *virgin, virgin*? Or just like a haven't-gone-*all-the-way* virgin?"

Jo stared at her blankly. "I have no idea what that means."

"*Oh my God!*" Kayleigh collapsed beside Jo and threw her arms over Jo's shoulders. "Leave my virgin roommate alone!"

"We should make that her nickname," murmured Addie.

"Totally nickname worthy," Liv agreed.

"You are not calling me *the virgin roommate*," Jo deadpanned. "Also, what about Miller? Doesn't he get a nickname?"

Addie and Liv exchanged another glance.

"The virgin hall mate?" Addie suggested.

"Virgin boy?" said Liv.

Miller cleared his throat. "Yeah, I think I'll pass on the nickname too."

Liv waved her finger between them. "Y'all should just fuck. Two birds with one stone and all that."

"Oh my God!" Kayleigh threw her arms up. "Okay, moving on. I'm going."

Another few rounds through the circle and a second empty box of Lime-a-ritas later, Addie and Liv were practically flat on the ground. Their legs were stretched out in the middle of the circle so only their heads were propped against Kayleigh's bed. Their eyes flitted around the room under half-closed lids.

"Maybe we should get them next door," mumbled Jo under her breath.

Addie whispered something to Liv, and the two broke out in hysterical laughter, clutching hands and kicking their feet, crushing what was left of the bag of chips in their wake.

"I'm *fineeee*," said Addie as she struggled to sit up. After several failed, flailing attempts, she managed to pull herself to her feet, only to sway so violently that she fell against

Kayleigh's bed. "It's *her* you need to worry about." She pointed at Liv's prone form on the floor.

"I've got it," Kayleigh muttered as she hefted herself up.

Liv didn't move as Kayleigh and Addie each wrestled an arm under her shoulders and dragged her toward the door. As they crossed into the suite's common area, Liv's head popped up.

"Oh, God," muttered Miller.

The room filled with Addie's shrieks as the girls frantically pivoted toward the bathroom. The door slammed behind them, but the sound of Liv's retching still seeped through loud and clear.

Jo and Miller sat there as the toilet flushed and Addie disappeared into her side of the suite, only to duck back into the bathroom a moment later with a fresh T-shirt in her hands.

"I wouldn't let them get to you," Miller said after a minute.

Jo glanced at him.

"With the virgin and band guy comments," he explained. "Just—any guy who's worth your time isn't going to, uh, pressure you into anything, you know?" He shrugged and looked away as the smallest trace of red snuck up the side of his neck.

A slow smile crept onto her face, and she bumped her shoulder against his. "What do you think are the odds they'll let those nicknames go?"

He chuckled. "Not a chance."

❧ 4 ❧

SENIOR YEAR - MARCH

Jo PINCHED HER LEG UNDER HER DESK AND FORCED HER eyes to refocus on the board. Usually her graphic design classes were pretty interesting, but this history of graphic design elective had been Miller's idea, and she'd give just about anything to be anywhere else. In retrospect, it was her own fault. She should've known someone who willingly sat through law classes was not to be trusted.

Jordan's glasses swam into view, and he winked at her. Jo quickly dropped her eyes and pretended to take notes.

Great. Now Jordan was going to think she'd been staring at him and was still interested, which couldn't be further from the truth. In fact, he'd been the most boring fling she'd had since she lost her virginity freshman year—and there had been a many interesting stories in between.

"Now I know graduation is just a mere two months away for all you seniors," called Dr. Wells. "But *please* don't make me hunt you down for these papers or make me read something you wrote at three in the morning after one-dollar shooters at college night. They're due next Tuesday at midnight. All right. We'll pick up here on Monday. Don't forget the new TA office hours are on Thursday." He patted Jordan on the back.

The room immediately filled with noise as everyone shoved belongings into bags and scraped their chairs back. Jordan started heading up the steps toward them, and Jo urgently jabbed Miller beside her to move faster.

"I thought you said you ended things with Teacher's Pet for good," mumbled Miller as they shuffled toward the door.

"Oh, I did." Jo pointedly avoided looking at the front of the room until they escaped into the hall.

Miller quirked an eyebrow. "Does he know that?"

"Don't start with me." Jo swatted him in the chest. "I'm not here to coddle feelings. If adult men can't learn to take a hint and move on, that's not on me."

Jo turned toward the parking lot without warning, and Miller immediately fell into step beside her.

"What was the *hint* this time?" he asked.

"After nearly falling asleep while he was still inside me, I told him I wasn't interested in anything more than a hookup, and we should probably just see other people. Then I left and stopped responding to his texts. You can't get much clearer than that."

Miller snorted out a laugh. "Glad to hear you haven't lost your knack for sensitivity."

"I just have zero tolerance for bullshit." Jo wound through the parking lot, incessantly hitting the panic button on her keys, trying to locate her car in the over-crowded lot. People streamed past them in the opposite direction, heading to the academic buildings for the next class block. Finally, her Jeep let out a series of angry beeps at the end of the row.

"Don't you have another class right now?" Miller asked.

"I dropped it." Jo's hand clamped around the handle to the driver's side door, and she grinned at him over her shoulder. "Don't *you* have a class right now?"

"I'm *going* to drop it."

"I knew I was a bad influence on you." Jo did a quick sweep of her reflection in the window as Miller circled to the passenger side. She'd thought her orange tube top complimented her red hair this morning, but now she was seeing it with entirely new eyes in the natural lighting. Maybe if she threw her hair into a ponytail, it would help. Miller slid into his seat, the top of his head nearly skimming the roof of the car. He leaned over and knocked on the window in front of her face.

"Get in, Palmer. You look great."

She half expected his diplomatic smile—perfectly straight white teeth and dimples—but the smile he gave her through the glass was quieter. The barest curl of his lips, just on the one side.

She threw the door open with a sigh and tossed her backpack into his lap. Accustomed to the routine, Miller caught it with ease and tucked it beside his feet. Just as she planted a foot on the door to haul herself inside, Jo felt a tap on her shoulder.

She whipped around and let out a small squeak of surprise.

Mere inches behind her stood Jordan, slightly out of breath, his shaggy blonde hair even messier than usual.

Well, shit.

"Hey," he said, eyes flickering from Jo to Miller behind her.

"Jordan." Jo glanced around them and raised her eyebrows. "Did I forget something in the lecture hall?"

"Oh, no, no, nothing like that. I just wanted to ask you something."

Jo cleared her throat and forced herself to think through her next words instead of letting the first thing that came to mind spew out. Not that she particularly cared for Jordan's feelings, especially since he was just being plain stupid at this point, but they did have an audience, and she didn't want to wound his pride any more than necessary. But then again, maybe that's what it would take for him to finally leave her alone.

"You know, Jordan—"

"I heard you're coming to the cocktail tonight," he continued as if she hadn't spoken. "I know you'll be working and everything, but Daniel did say you were allowed a plus-one if you wanted. I mean, I know I'm not technically a *plus*-one since I'm a brother and I'll be there anyway, but—"

"You know, it's great luck that you're here, man." Miller appeared at Jo's side, threw his arm around her shoulders, and pulled her tightly against him. The scent of his after-shave momentarily flooded her senses. "I don't think either of us managed to write down the reading. Was it chapters three through twelve?"

Jordan's entire expression shifted as he took in Miller's towering height. His eyes shifted to the place where Miller's chest was touching Jo's shoulder.

Finally coming out of her shock, Jo leaned into Miller and gave Jordan an innocent smile. "Thanks, Jordan, I really appreciate it. But, uh, Miller is actually my date for tonight!"

Jordan paused for a moment, eyes flickering between the two of them as he took this in. He didn't look nearly as dissuaded by this as Jo had hoped. "Oh. Well, I'm sure Miller wouldn't mind, right? I mean, it's not like he'd be a real date anyway."

"Not a real date?" Miller asked.

"Yeah, you know." Jordan shifted his weight. "I mean, I know you two go as friends to a ton of stuff, but this is one of our last cocktails, so—"

Miller didn't blink. "Well, we weren't planning on going as friends."

"Oh." Jordan didn't seem to quite know what to make of this. His eyes searched Jo's face for an explanation, but she just shrugged and leaned farther into Miller's chest.

"Right. Cool. Great." Jordan's expression hardened, then he started backtracking, putting several feet of distance between them. "Guess I'll see you guys there, then."

"See you, man." Miller waved, expression entirely friendly. He waited until Jordan turned and disappeared behind the next row of cars before dropping his arm.

Jo practically collapsed against the side of her Jeep as all of the air fled from her lungs. She met Miller's gaze as his face transformed into a devilish grin.

"Thank you," she conceded. "You don't have to be annoying about it."

He shrugged and headed back to his seat. "Whatever you say, *darling.*"

"Since I'm driving, you realize you're completely at my mercy," said Jo as she started the car. "Which means you have to be nice to me."

"It's my turn to buy the fries, so we both know you're not leaving me behind." He stretched back in his seat—perpetually set back at the farthest setting to accommodate his long legs—and flipped on the radio.

All it took was a single note for Jo to recognize the song. Miller lurched up in his seat.

Johanna by *United Fates* scrolled across the screen.

"Shit," Miller muttered. He reached for the knob to change the station but ended up turning up the volume. "*Shit.*" He slammed his hand against the buttons, turning the radio off all together.

They sat in silence for several moments, Jo's hands tightly fisted around the steering wheel. She stared at the line of cars straight ahead, her vision blurring around the edges. Finally, she said, "I can't believe they still play that fucking song."

"And they haven't made a decent one since."

Jo sucked in a long, slow breath before glancing at him sideways. "You're buying me an extra-large fry today."

JO SHOWED UP TO THE COCKTAIL AN HOUR EARLY TO check out the venue and set up her equipment. *Cocktail* may have even been too generous of a word. It was at a Mexican restaurant that had a bar in the back. Granted, they had a huge patio with a pretty nice view, and they'd strung up some colorful lantern lights to make it look more festive. It wasn't the worst frat cocktail location she'd seen.

Miller grumbled as he shadowed her, going on about how *of all the frats, why did it have to be Tri Chi?* Miller had never been much of a fan of the frats, which was slightly ironic, seeing as they all seemed to love him.

"You're the one who offered yourself up as my date," Jo reminded him as she took some practice shots on the patio to test the lighting. She'd been surprised when Daniel, Tri Chi's president, emailed her a few weeks ago, asking her to be the photographer for the event. But apparently some big shot in their fraternity was in town, someone high up— Jo had no clue how the whole system worked, nor did she care. All she knew was they were giving her three hundred bucks for the night, *and* all the free food and drinks she could manage. "So you have no one but yourself to blame. Hey, jump in this shot for me, would you?"

Miller sighed and sauntered into frame. His dark hair was getting longer, long enough that he repeatedly had to push it back to keep it out of his face. Despite all of his protests, he'd dressed up for the occasion, sporting fitted gray pants and a classic white button-down with the sleeves rolled up to his elbows. He left the shirt open at the collar, exposing the long column of his throat, as he balanced a hand on the deck's railing, propped one foot out to the side, and threw his head back in a dramatic pose.

"You're buying me a beer," he announced.

"It's an open bar."

"Then you're buying me two beers."

Jo inspected the pictures on her camera's screen, and Miller ambled back to peer at them over her shoulder. "I should've been a model," he mused.

"I think you should stick with law school."

He squinted at her. "I can't tell if that was supposed to be an insult."

"I didn't expect to see you two here."

Miller stiffened, and Jo hesitated a moment before turning around.

Foster. Of course she'd known he'd be here, but Tri Chi was a big enough frat there'd been a chance she wouldn't have to see him.

Well, she'd *thought* she had a chance.

He was wearing a gaudy red suit; red, white, and blue socks; and a matching tie. Judging by the haze in his eyes, even though the cocktail hadn't started yet, *his* night certainly had.

"I'm working, Foster." Jo held up her camera for emphasis. "You couldn't find a date?"

A girl in a shiny white slip dress appeared at his side and tucked herself under his arm, her eyes as glassy as his were. Her blonde hair was neatly arranged in a crown of braids atop her head. Honestly, she looked stunning.

Not that Jo was going to tell her that.

"Hi, Addie," she offered.

Addie looked her up and down, then flicked her gaze to Miller. "I guess some things never change, huh?"

Jo raised her eyebrows at the two of them. "Clearly. Now, if you'll excuse us." She grabbed Miller's sleeve and pulled him toward the bar. "Have fun tonight, guys!" she called over her shoulder, right before taking a picture at a very unflattering angle.

"That one's a keeper for sure." Miller nodded at the camera screen.

"I'm thinking it would do well on the Greek life home page."

Miller snorted and nodded at the bartender as they slipped back inside the restaurant. "Are you allowed to drink on the job?"

"I agreed to nothing that said otherwise."

"You want a beer?"

Jo waved over the bartender. "Two whiskeys."

Miller let out a low whistle. "So you're trying to kill me tonight."

Jo watched Foster and Addie through the window as Foster not so subtly slipped a joint out of his pocket, and the two went in for a sloppy kiss. Foster immediately slid his hands down, trying to find purchase under her skirt. "To think we ever lived with them," she muttered.

"It's a miracle we made it out of freshman year alive," said Miller.

Jo raised her glass. "Cheers to that."

THE DROWSY ENERGY OF THE PARTY SLOWLY SHARPENED as more bodies poured through the doors, the air filling with laughter, high fives, and the clink of high heels against the floor. A buffet was set up in the center of the restaurant, where most of the younger brothers and their dates gathered, piling their plates high with nachos and burritos. Anyone who was old enough to drink immediately headed for the bar in the back and ventured outside to the patio. Jo and Miller lingered off to the side, sipping their drinks and sharing a plate of chips, Jo dutifully snapping away on her camera.

Once people caught on to why Jo was there, groups rushed up to her, begging her to take their pictures. And that's how the entire first hour went—guys holding up beers, arms thrown around one another's shoulders, girls hanging off their dates with hair properly fluffed or thrown back. Once Jo had enough pictures to satisfy Daniel, she tucked the camera back into its bag and slung it over her shoulder.

"Here, I'll take it," offered Miller.

They ordered a round of Manhattans from the bar and ventured back onto the patio, now bustling with activity. Salsa music blared from the speakers, and a girl in a floor-length red dress was attempting to teach a group how to properly do the dance.

"Oh!" Jo jostled Miller's arm. "I want to learn!"

He gestured toward the group. "Go on, then."

"Absolutely not." She grabbed his wrist and dragged him along. "If I'm dancing, you're dancing."

"Jo, I'm serious—"

"One dance, Mill, *please?* I need a partner."

Miller sighed and glanced over his shoulder, probably looking for an escape route. But then he whipped around, seized Jo's hand, and spun her toward him. Before she could react, he twirled her out again, his steps perfectly in sync with the music, his movements fluid. He pulled her against his chest one final time, one hand in hers, the other secure on her waist. She locked eyes with him, a little out of breath, and could feel his pulse hammering in his wrist.

As he released her, a group of onlookers erupted in applause.

"Don't ask me why I know how to do that," he said lowly.

Jo stared at him, momentarily speechless, as he retrieved their discarded drinks from a nearby table and held one out to her.

She grinned as she took it. "You are by far the best date I've ever had."

He winked. "I better be."

"Mind if I cut in?" Jordan stumbled between them and bumped into Jo hard enough that she fell back a step, her drink sloshing over the side of her cup.

"Dude," said Miller.

"Sorry, man. I just tripped."

Jo wiped the liquid from her arm. "You're drunk."

Jordan scoffed, swayed on his feet, then steadied himself on a nearby table. He was wearing a white button-down shirt nearly identical to Miller's, though his now had a large brown stain from Jo's drink. "Everyone here's drunk," slurred Jordan.

"Let's get you a DD," offered Jo.

"Not until we've had our dance."

Jo rolled her eyes toward the starry night above them. Even drunk, he surely had to hear how much he sounded like a petulant child.

"Come on, dude," Miller cut in. "It's not going to happen."

Jordan got right in Miller's face, so close their noses almost touched. Miller, to his credit, showed no reaction to this. "I didn't realize you spoke for her now, *dude*."

"Jordan, please," Jo said quietly. "You're making a scene."

There were at least a dozen onlookers at this point, half of which were other members of Jordan's fraternity. Jo shot them an exasperated look, but none of his *brothers* deemed it necessary to step in.

"You really think anyone here is buying this act?" He flicked his wrist toward Miller. "We all know you friend-zoned him a long time ago. It's just insulting, is what it is. For you to bring him to *my* frat. Or maybe it's just pathetic. You couldn't even find a real date. Guess that's not surprising. With the way you get around, you should have a health advisory on your forehead—"

Miller's fist landed straight across his jaw. Someone gasped as Jordan's body hit the floor. He grabbed a table-cloth on his way down, sending glasses shattering against the patio. The music cut off as Jordan spit and climbed to his hands and knees.

Miller stepped over the mess and took Jo's hand, his face entirely blank. But as calm as he looked on the outside, his hand was shaking. Jo stared at him, her entire body frozen in shock.

"Get that bitch out of here," Jordan spat.

Miller surged toward him, but this time, the surrounding guys finally jumped in, some grabbing Miller and hauling him back, the others jumping in front of Jordan.

"What the fuck?" The door to the restaurant flew open, and Daniel, the fraternity's president, stormed over. He looked from Jordan on the ground, to the guys holding Miller back, to Jo. "What's going on?" His question, apparently, was directed at her.

Jo stared at him, wide-eyed. "He—I—"

"Jordan's drunk," muttered one of the others. "He needs to go home."

"We were just leaving too." Miller shook off the guys holding his arms and took Jo's hand again. "You ready?"

Jo nodded, mute, and shards of glass crunched under her heels as she followed him out the door. She glanced over her shoulder to see Jordan shoving away anyone who tried to help him up.

Miller was silent as they slid into an Uber. Jo stared at the side of his face, but he kept his gaze trained on his hands in his lap.

"Mill," she whispered.

"I'm sorry," he said at the same time. "I don't know what came over me back there—I shouldn't have—I'm sorry."

She reached over and lightly touched his arm. "Is your hand okay?"

He snorted out a laugh. "Believe it or not, his head is a lot harder than the punching bags."

"Oh I definitely believe it."

They lapsed back into silence as the Uber turned up the street to the college's apartment buildings, the AC humming lowly in the background. Jo stared out the window, trying to think of something to say, but the shock was like a barricade in her mind, blocking out everything else. She glanced down at Miller's hands, and despite the darkness, she could make out a slight tremor in his fingers. She slid across the seat, wrapped her hands around his arm, and rested her head on his shoulder. "Thanks for coming tonight," she murmured into his sleeve. "I'd been looking for an excuse to leave anyway."

He laughed and rested his cheek on the top of her head. "Happy to be of service."

5

FRESHMAN YEAR - SEPTEMBER

JOHANNA SPUN AROUND IN FRONT OF THE MIRROR IN A strapless bra and high-waisted jeans, her hair piled into a messy topknot. She raised two shirts, holding each to her body briefly. "Which one?"

Kayleigh squinted down at her from her lofted bed. "I vote the lacy black tank. You could just tuck in the front—very classy. It's in all the fashion blogs right now."

"Miller?" Johanna spun to face his chair in the corner, where he was pointedly not looking at her. "Which shirt?"

"Either one as long as you *put one on.*"

"You're no help," she muttered as she slipped Kayleigh's choice over her head. After quickly applying a coat of lip gloss, she turned away from the mirror, refusing to allow herself any more time. The more time she spent in front of the mirror, the more she cared about this date. And the more she cared, the more nervous she'd be.

"You look perfect," said Kayleigh. Well, that's what Jo

thought she said. Her words were entirely drowned out by the shrieks of laughter coming from Addie and Liv's room, something that was quickly becoming the ever-present background track in their suite.

"Are you dressed yet?" asked Miller, a hand full-on covering his eyes now.

"Yes, Miller, I'm decent."

He lowered his hand, did a quick appraisal of her outfit, and nodded.

"That's all I get?" Jo demanded.

Miller threw his hands up. "You already know you look hot. You don't need me to tell you."

Kayleigh climbed to the other end of her bed and glanced out the window as Jo searched the ground for the right pair of shoes. Grey hadn't told her what they'd be doing tonight, so she didn't know if flats or heels were the way to go. She settled on a pair of strappy wedges and balanced herself on Miller's shoulder as she did the clasps. He sighed as if this were a major inconvenience.

"What the hell?" said Kayleigh. "Jo, I—I think your ride is here."

Jo shuffled over to peek out the window and let out a small gasp. A gigantic bus was parked outside their dorm, practically blocking the entire street. UNITED FATES was plastered across the side in thick, red letters.

"Subtle," she muttered.

Miller appeared at her side and craned his neck to see. "Is he planning to kidnap you and take you on tour?"

The door to the bus swung open and Grey stepped out on the sidewalk in black jeans, a black T-shirt, and a black leather jacket. Johanna would be rolling her eyes at the whole cliché of it all if it didn't look so damn good on him. He glanced both ways down the street, then tilted his head back to take in the building.

"Get away from the window!" Jo shrilled, grabbing Miller's sleeve and pulling him down. They tripped over each other, landing in a tangle of limbs on the floor, as Kayleigh laughed at them from the bed. Jo splayed out on her back and stared at the ceiling for a second. "Is this a dumb idea?" she asked to no one in particular.

Miller settled in beside her and jabbed her lightly with his elbow. "Go have fun tonight. Worse comes to worse, you hate it, you call us, and we come pick you up."

She turned her head to look at him. He stared back at her with raised eyebrows. "He can't get in the building," he reminded her. "You're gonna have to go downstairs."

"Fuck." She looked back to the ceiling as her phone buzzed in her pocket—probably Grey letting her know he was here.

"It'll be fun!" Kayleigh assured her. "*And* he's really hot."

"Right." Jo climbed to her feet, brushed off her jeans, and checked her hair one final time in the mirror. She looked her reflection in the eye and whispered, "It'll be fun."

GREY BEAMED AS JOHANNA STEPPED ONTO THE SIDEWALK and headed toward him. He was clean-shaven tonight, his hair purposefully disheveled and brushed up in the front. Her chest tightened to an almost painful degree, but she couldn't pinpoint the exact cause. Nerves? Excitement? Anticipation? Whatever it was, she hoped it didn't show on her face and tried to brush it off as she asked, "Did your car break down or something?"

He held out a hand, still smiling. She hesitated, very much aware of the people gawking at them from across the street, but she took it. He led her up the stairs with a hand braced on her lower back. It was larger inside than she'd first thought. There was a black leather couch on one side and a full bar on the other. Two TVs hung high on the walls, along with various light fixtures that reflected off the surrounding glossy surfaces. Grey led her down the aisle to a small table and two black leather booths.

"The bus is new," he explained. "We're going on tour later this year, and I've been looking for an excuse to take it out."

"So, I'm the excuse?" she asked.

"An excuse who looks absolutely stunning tonight, I may add. Come on, I'll give you the full tour." He led her farther back, still holding on to her hand, pointing to things and explaining as he went. Past the table, there was a sliding door that opened up to the sleeping quarters. Two sets of bunk beds lined the walls, and in the very back, an enormous king-size bed swallowed the rest of the space. Cabinets were nestled basically anywhere they could fit for more storage—under the beds, above the beds, tucked into corners. The same kind of lights that were on the floors of a movie theater snaked around the roof of the bus and framed the windows.

Jo dropped his hand and gestured around them. "So is the bus the destination, or is the bus taking us somewhere?"

Half of Grey's mouth curved into a smile as he twisted some knobs in the wall. Light jazz music poured into the small space, and Johanna couldn't stop herself from laughing.

"Not a fan of jazz?" asked Grey.

"No, it's not that." Jo plopped down on the couch. "It's just, let me guess. Next you're going to dim the lights."

"Well, we do have some great mood lighting in here."

"I noticed."

Grey paced back to the front of the bus and knocked on the wall. "We're all good in here, Chuck!" he called.

The bus rumbled to life, and Jo lurched forward as it pulled away from the curb. Grey took a place on the couch a respectful distance away, leaned his head back against the window, and closed his eyes. "How can you not like jazz?" he murmured. "Brilliant stuff."

Lights from the street flickered across his face as they drove, highlighting the stubble along his jaw, the angles of his cheekbones, the long column of his throat. His sweeping eyelashes looked even longer than usual against his cheeks, and there was a softness to his features she hadn't seen before.

Johanna realized she was staring and quickly looked away before he could open his eyes and notice too.

"I never said I don't like jazz," she said.

Grey's eyes flickered open, and he leaned his head to the side to look at her. "So, what do you think of the bus? I imagine it's about the same amount of space as a freshman dorm." Jo narrowed her eyes, and a bemused smile rose to his lips. "I may have Facebook stalked you," he explained. "I'll have you know, fake IDs are illegal in the great state of Oregon."

Jo snorted. "I think they're illegal anywhere. Are you secretly taking me to the police station?"

"Quite the contrary. If you hadn't showed up in that bar, we never would've met. And what a shame that would've been."

She met his gaze, and the intensity behind his eyes made her cheeks flush with heat. She turned to look back outside. "You're still not telling me where we're going?"

He closed his eyes and settled against the window. "Why would I want to ruin the surprise?"

"Can I have a hint?"

That same damn smile returned. "You're quite the impatient one, aren't you?"

"I don't think it's an unreasonable question."

"Unreasonable? No." One eye opened. "But I'm still not going to tell you."

Johanna let out a long, dramatic sigh, leaned back on the couch, and propped her feet in Grey's lap. "Fine. I suppose you can just wake me up when we're there, then."

He had the kind of laugh that could fill a room—throaty and deep. He wrapped his hands around her ankles and gave them a gentle squeeze. "I think you and I are going to get along just fine, Johanna."

THE BUS TOOK THEM STRAIGHT PAST THE CITY AND down a backroad she hadn't even known was there. The leaves were already starting to shift into fall, framing their drive with gold and red on either side. She'd been trailing the setting sun through the window when a wooden sign popped up on their left, too fast for her to read the name of the campsite before they turned onto a dirt road.

"You're not seriously taking me camping, are you?" she demanded.

"I don't think either of us look like the camping type."

Several over vehicles and camper vans swam into view as the bus continued toward the edge of a cliff. It pulled off into the only remaining parking spot in the lot.

Grey offered her his hand as they climbed out of the bus, and he led her toward the tree line. There had to be at least a dozen other people there, all of whom whooped at the sight of Grey. He high-fived and nodded as they passed, but he didn't stop. He continued to lead Jo toward the trees, murmuring, "We'll do introductions in a bit."

She heard the roar of the fire before she saw it. Nestled near the edge of the cliff sat a generous bonfire, surrounded by large stones and fallen tree trunks for seating. They paused beside it, and Johanna couldn't help but stare off the edge of the cliff—cliff being an extremely generous term since these mountains severely paled in comparison to the ones she was used to back home in Colorado—but the sun setting behind the hills in the distance was certainly nothing to scoff at. Electric hues of orange and pink bled across the sky, tinging the entire world red around them.

"So." Grey stepped up beside her and tucked his hands in his pockets. "What do you think? Will this do?"

She leaned her shoulder against his. "Better than the dive bar, I'll give you that."

He grinned, and the flickering light from the fire flashed off his profile. "I'll take it. You want to come meet the rest of the band?" He escorted her back through the trees, one hand steady against the small of her back. Their first stop was at a cooler to grab a couple of beers—*thank God*. A man and a woman nearby inched over as Grey popped the top off a bottle and handed it to Jo.

"You must be the famous Johanna," said the man. He was almost exactly the same height as Grey, but that was where the similarities ended. Where Grey was all angles and hard lines, this man had a round face and boyish smile. He held out a large hand for her to shake. "I'm Eric, United Fates' manager. And this is my lovely wife, Gwen."

Jo had to force her eyes not to bulge at the word *wife*. How old were these people? How old did they think *she* was? She shook his hand and smiled at Gwen, who didn't look much older than Johanna was with her short, black bob and sparkly eyeshadow.

"Famous, huh?" Jo asked, glancing at Grey out of the corner of her eye. "Should I be concerned?"

Eric clapped Grey on the back and winked. "Very."

"Isn't it past your bedtime, Eric?" Grey asked.

"Ah, yes, pick on the old people." Eric threw his arm around Gwen's shoulders and steered them in the opposite direction. "Believe it or not, one day soon, you, too, will be twenty-eight. Have fun tonight, kids."

Grey smirked and nodded toward a man leaning against a tree a few yards away. "That's Pete over there—he plays bass. Eric is his older brother." He made the rounds, pointing out and naming the rest of the people in the clearing. "I'd take you over to introduce everyone," he murmured, suddenly standing right behind her. "But they're all notoriously chatty." His hands found her waist, and his chest pressed against her back. "And I'd much rather have you to myself. Especially if I'm still on that one-hour time limit."

Jo laughed, and her cheeks warmed at how breathless it came out. "Considering you ate up twenty-five minutes getting here, and it'll take twenty-five minutes to get me home, that would leave you with…ten minutes."

His lips brushed the back of her ear, and she felt his breath on the back of her neck. "Would you be oh-so generous, Johanna, to allow me a little more time tonight?"

She took a swig of her beer, pretending to consider this, and leaned back a little against his chest. "Only if you make it worth my while."

ONCE THE LAST OF THE LIGHT DRAINED FROM THE SKY and the temperature plummeted, everyone crowded around the fire. Jo and Grey claimed the log facing the cliff as the rest of the group loitered near the edge, laughing and tipping back cans of beer. One of the girls came around and held out a bag of marshmallows to Jo, though her eyes were on Grey as Jo reached inside and pulled two out to roast. The girl walked away and joined the rest of the crowd wordlessly. Grey hadn't introduced Jo to anyone else, and none of them had tried to come over. Jo shivered and wrapped her arms around herself.

"Here," Grey murmured as he slipped his leather jacket around her shoulders. She nestled into his side, but refused to look at him despite feeling the heat of his gaze on her face. Instead, she stabbed a long stick through the marshmallow and leaned forward to hold it over the fire.

"I'm sorry about all of them," he added after a minute. "They can be...unwelcoming sometimes, especially when they're all drunk. It really isn't personal."

She glanced at him out of the corner of her eye, and he stared back, his expression serious. "But they're your friends," she said slowly.

He inclined his head, but pressed his lips together like maybe that wasn't exactly true.

She turned back to the fire, focusing on getting the perfect brown edges on her marshmallow in hopes that it would distract her from the twisting in the pit of her stomach. It wasn't the *not* talking that bothered her. Well, not entirely. It was the looks she'd catch them shooting over their shoulders. The whispers they shared after they looked away.

Grey met her eyes again. A small, soft smile crossed his face, and she realized she was probably making a big deal out of nothing. Seeing into things that weren't even there.

Maybe they were just trying not to intrude on her date with him.

The fire crackled, filling the air around them with smoke. Grey reached over and brushed a hand against her thigh as he angled his head back to look at the stars. They weren't far enough removed from the city for a completely clear view, but the stars were much brighter here than Jo could see from her dorm. She studied Grey's profile, the soft set of his features when he thought no one was looking.

Once the marshmallow was properly roasted, Grey pulled it off the stick and smashed it between two graham crackers for her. She quickly took a bite to keep the gooey marshmallow from dripping, but all that accomplished was smearing it on her face.

"I'm very classy," she said around a mouthful.

Grey smiled and leaned in until he was just inches away, so close she could see the dance of the flames reflected in his eyes. His gaze flickered to her lips, just for a moment, and his smile shifted into something much less innocent. He crossed the rest of the distance between them, but instead of his mouth finding hers, he leaned down and slowly licked the marshmallow off her chin. He leaned back just enough to look into Jo's eyes, and she licked the remaining crumbs from her lips, every nerve in her body suddenly warm.

He reached up, cupped the side of her face with his palm, and slowly brushed her lips with his thumb. Her breath caught in her throat as he leaned forward again. Her eyes fluttered shut as she waited to feel his lips against hers, but...it didn't come.

She blinked her eyes open just in time to see a slow smile spread across his lips. Then it hit her—he was toying with her. He was *enjoying* whatever this game was, probably just to watch her squirm. She was about to pull back when he slid his hand up her thigh, and he leaned forward again, this time crushing his mouth to hers before she could even think about it.

She stayed stiff for a moment, more confused than anything else. But then his teeth dug into her lower lip, and the taste of him filled her mouth—beer and smoke and chocolate—and despite the small voice in the back of Jo's mind reminding her they were surrounded by his friends, as his hands slid under the hem of her shirt and found the bare skin of her back, she melted into his chest. It was nothing like the clumsy kisses she'd had before. Every movement was sure and measured. Every sweep of his tongue, every graze of his teeth. She gasped, breathing in the breath he was breathing out, marveling in the heat of his hands as they traveled across her skin. And she realized every part of this was deliberate—every pause, every touch —it was like a game to him. A perfectly choreographed routine.

And for some reason, she didn't want it to stop.

"You want to go grab another beer?" he murmured against her mouth.

Unable to speak, she nodded. She wasn't sure if he actually wanted a beer or just an excuse to leave, and she found a small part of herself hoping for the latter. If people turned to look as they left, Jo didn't notice. Grey adjusted his jacket on her shoulders as they stood, then took her hand as he led her back through the trees. The air was noticeably colder now that they were away from the fire, and she huddled against his arm for warmth. He went straight past the clearing with the cooler and toward the parking lot, and Johanna's stomach flipped.

"Don't tell anyone," he murmured. "But I have much better beer in the bus."

He didn't turn on the overhead lights as they climbed inside, leaving only the movie theater strips to light the way. He pulled two beers from the mini fridge—a brand Jo had never heard of before—but didn't let go of her hand. He set the beers on the bar and pulled her closer until she was standing just inches away from his chest.

"I think the beers can wait, don't you?" he asked.

She barely had time to nod before he pinned her against the wall and covered her mouth with his. His teeth dug into her bottom lip as he yanked the jacket from her shoulders and tossed it aside. She started to trace her hands up his chest, but he grabbed her wrists and pulled them above her head. Every nerve in her body was on fire and desperate for contact, and she arched against him. He pulled her away from the wall, spinning them both around so he was sitting on the couch and she was straddling his lap.

As his lips trailed down her jaw, he let his teeth scrape along the side of her throat. She tilted her head to the side, granting him better access, her breaths seeming so much louder now in the quiet. His hands held her firmly on his lap, then slowly trailed up her hips, finding the sliver of skin between her jeans and the hem of her shirt.

Finally, she managed to catch her breath. Everything was happening so fast, too fast, like the room was spinning. She could only half remember how she'd gotten there. She pressed her hands against his chest and pushed back, just an inch. He licked his lips as he looked up at her.

"Not tonight," she breathed. "I don't want to do this—not tonight."

"Okay." One of his hands slid up her back and rested just behind her neck. "But does that mean I have to stop kissing you?"

She bit her lip and slowly shook her head.

His hold on her tightened, and the smile that overtook his face was feral. "Excellent."

❧ 6 ❧

SENIOR YEAR - MARCH

"JO, WE REALLY NEED TO TALK ABOUT YOUR TASTE IN hookups." Miller strode into the newspaper office even more disheveled than usual. His navy button-down was wrinkled and half tucked into his jeans, his hair sticking straight up on one side.

Luckily, it was still half an hour before the meeting, so no one else had shown up yet. Jo was sitting at the front of the room, feet propped on the table, scarfing down her microwavable lunch while she studied for a graphic design quiz. Mustering any motivation when graduation was so close was nearly impossible, and Jo's eyes kept drifting from her textbook to the window at the back of the room. It was a perfectly sunny day, and the back quad was flooded with people laying out on blankets or throwing Frisbees around. She could probably get some good shots—

Miller slammed a piece of paper on the desk in front of her and pointed at it.

"What am I looking at?" she asked without actually looking at it.

"What grade did you get on your paper for Wells' class?"

She shrugged. "A *B*.'"

"*Look.*"

Sighing, Jo let her feet fall to the floor and leaned forward. "*Yikes.*" A large, red *F* was scrawled at the top of Miller's page. Jo did a quick scan of his opening paragraph and frowned. "Wait, this is way better than mine—ohhh. Jordan."

Miller snatched the paper back. "Yeah, *oh*."

Jo drew her shoulders up to her ears and grimaced. "You should go talk to Professor Wells. The second he reads your paper, he'll know that isn't the grade you deserved. I'll go with you and explain things, if you want."

Miller shoved the paper back in his bag. "I'll go during his office hours later. How stupid does Jordan have to be to think I *wouldn't* talk to Wells?"

Jo perked up. "Maybe he'll get fired. Can TAs get fired?"

"I hope so," muttered Miller as he pulled up another chair and collapsed next to Jo. He glanced at her sideways. "You know that's supposed to be my chair, right?"

She spun around in a circle. "But it's the only one that swivels."

"Which is why it's the *Editor in Chief's* chair."

"Well, today it's the *Photography Director's* chair."

Miller shook his head, but even as he turned his back to dig through his bag, she could tell he was smiling. He whipped out a folder and tossed it on the table. "Do you have those layouts for me, *Photography Director?*"

Jo slouched a little lower in the chair. "Don't you have anything better to do than haggle me on my lunch break?"

Miller gave her a pointed look. "Jo, our final issue is coming up, not to mention the final showcase—"

"*Please* don't remind me. My parents are flying in for that." She pursed her lips. "Well, so they say. We'll wait to see if they cancel last minute. And you *know* I'll have the issue ready in time. I always do."

Miller eyed the napkin where Jo had discarded the mushrooms from her lunch. "Are you going to eat those?"

"Ew, obviously not."

Miller shrugged and pulled the napkin toward him. "How's your portfolio coming? Think you'll have it ready in time for the showcase?"

Jo sucked her teeth. "It's fine as it is, I guess. I'm doing a shoot with that cool yoga studio by the lake this afternoon. So hopefully I can get those shots ready in time. But if not..." She flung her head back and stared at the ceiling. "Mediocre may have to do."

Miller snorted. "Your portfolio is hardly mediocre."

"But it's not *outstanding*, which is what I'll need to grab the attention of all the magazines and recruiters coming for the showcase. Did I tell you *Sandra Simone* is coming?"

Miller popped a mushroom into his mouth. "That photographer you've been salivating over for the past year?"

"I would *kill* to work with her after we graduate. I'd be an unpaid intern, a personal assistant, certified bitch-boy, *anything.* I need to figure out some way to stand out at the showcase."

Miller nudged her with his elbow. "You want me to pretend to be a crazy fan to impress her?"

Jo snorted and stabbed a carrot with her fork. "Only if you cry and make it look really realistic."

"I hate to brag, but I *did* take an acting class my freshman year of high school."

"Oh, wow. So you're clearly the most qualified for the position." Jo tilted her head back and batted her eyelashes. "Whatever would it take to convince you to help me?"

He shrugged and ate another mushroom. "I'd have conditions for the agreement, obviously."

"Obviously. Name your terms."

"One"—he held up a finger—"you're buying the fries for the rest of the semester."

She inclined her head. "Fair enough."

"Two, you have to be my date to that god-awful formal I have to attend with the rest of the Criminal Justice department."

She waved a hand. "I already assumed as much. Continue."

"And finally." Miller paused, his eyes squinting as if debating his next words. "You have to get *the fuck* out of my chair."

Jo lingered behind as the meeting wrapped up and the room filled with the sounds of shuffling papers and scraping chairs. There was a class block right after this, so most people had places to get to. Since Jo was nearly done with all of her credits already, her Monday/Wednesday/Friday schedule was pretty light aside from a morning seminar, these weekly meetings, and her independent study. The rest of the staff headed for the door, a much larger crowd now than it had been when she and Miller joined as freshmen. Ever since Miller took over the paper last year, their staff had multiplied—mostly of the female variety—which was a blessing and a curse. The paper was definitely better for it, and they were able to put out more content each week, but Jo's patience could do without as much human interaction and incessant questions from the clueless freshmen.

"Hey, Jo."

She turned at a tap on her shoulder. Gracie, one of their columnists, stood there with her teeth dug deep into her lower lip. Her curly blonde hair was yanked back in two tight space buns today, and they bounced along with every movement of her head.

Jo threw her backpack over one shoulder and her camera bag over the other. "What's up, Gracie?"

Gracie shifted her weight back and forth, seeming to grow more anxious by the second. Miller was still by the table at the front and met Jo's eyes over Gracie's head. He pinched his lips together to suppress the amused smile threatening to break out. Miller seemed to think it was hilarious that all of the freshmen were slightly terrified of Jo, but Jo really didn't get it. Sure, she found them a little exhausting to deal with, but she was always nice to them.

She couldn't judge them too harshly. Her freshman year had been...a trip, to say the least.

"Feel free to say no," said Gracie. "But I have to find a photographer to shadow for my Intro to Photography class, and I was wondering, well, if you wouldn't mind—"

"You free this afternoon?" asked Jo.

Gracie froze mid-word, her mouth hung wide, and blinked a few times before responding. "I—yes."

"Do you have a car?"

"Well, yeah—"

"Great." Jo patted her on the back and headed for the door. "You can drive me to my shoot."

Gracie hesitated only a moment before scurrying after Jo, who shot Miller a quick wave before slipping into the hallway. Jo slowed her walk just enough to hear Gracie's flip-flops frantically slapping against the ground behind her before shoving through the exit door and heading toward the quad.

"Which parking lot are you in?"

"I—we're going right now?" asked Gracie.

Jo finally paused and glanced at Gracie over her shoulder. The girl stood there panting, several strands now popping out of her buns. "Do you have something better to do?"

"I—no."

Jo was beginning to think Gracie started every sentence that way.

"It's in the west lot." Gracie pointed straight ahead. With a nod, Jo turned and continued across the quad, this time walking slowly enough that Gracie fell into step beside her.

"Who do you have for Intro?" asked Jo.

"Professor Sanders."

Jo grinned and fished around in her backpack for her sunglasses. "He's a riot. I think I still have my study guide from the final too, if you want it."

"That—that would be amazing." Gracie fisted her hands around her backpack, then dropped them to her sides, then regripped the straps again, not quite meeting Jo's eyes. "Did you have to do the shadowing project too?"

Jo bobbed her head. "The only photographer on campus I could find at the time was the old guy who did the ID badge portraits." She glanced at Gracie sideways. "I promise I will be *way* more fun than he was."

This, finally, made Gracie smile, though the rest of her features were still pinched together in what could only be described as sheer terror. Her Honda was in one of the first spots in the lot, parked perfectly in the center of the lines. As Jo climbed into the passenger seat, she glanced around in amazement. The entire interior gleamed like the car was brand new, no trace of clutter or mess to be found anywhere.

Gracie stared at her from the driver seat with wide eyes. "Is something wrong?"

"No!" Jo leaned back in the seat, breathing in the fresh, citrusy scent coming from the air freshener strapped to the shade over her head. "Your car is just so *clean*. Thank God we didn't take mine. You'd think I was a barbarian."

Gracie choked out a laugh that almost sounded painful as Jo punched the address into her phone's GPS. She leaned forward and attached it to the mount on Gracie's windshield so she could see. The car promptly fell into silence as Gracie pulled away from the school and headed for the interstate. Jo drummed her fingers against her knees, trying to figure out how to *not* be intimidating. She didn't think she was in the first place, but apparently, that was the problem.

"So are you a photography major too?" she tried.

"I'm still undecided. But I'm thinking a graphic design major with a photography minor."

"Oh, cool. I'm a photography major with a graphic design minor. You'll have to let me know if you need any recommendations for professors."

Gracie's shoulders relaxed a bit as they merged onto the highway. "That would actually be great. I don't know anyone else in either department."

"Cool. I'll give you my number later. But you'll have to remind me on your paper requirements since it's been a while since I did the shadowing project. Feel free to ask whatever during the shoot."

Gracie's eyes flickered from the phone to the road. "What is the shoot we're going to anyway?"

"Have you ever heard of Nature Yogis?"

"The yoga studio?"

"Yeah. I'm helping them with some marketing images —they shoot new ones with me every year. We're gonna start down by the lake, then get a few shots at their studio. They only booked me for two hours, so this shouldn't take too long. Do you have any photography experience?"

Gracie ducked her head a bit. "Besides taking pictures on my iPhone, not really."

Jo laughed and pointed to the gravel road that split off toward the lake. "What have you guys learned in class so far?"

The car jostled as they transitioned onto the gravel, and Gracie tightened her grip on the steering wheel. Both hands were clamped tightly enough that white split across her knuckles, and they were perfectly spaced at the ten and two marks of the clock the way driver's ed taught. Beads of sweat had formed on Gracie's forehead, and Jo's gut clenched a little. Maybe asking Gracie to drive hadn't been the casual favor she'd assumed it would be.

"Just the basics," Gracie finally said. "Aperture, shutter speeds—that kind of thing."

"You can pull in up there." Jo pointed to the parking lot ahead where several cars were waiting. She waved through the window at Brenda, the studio's owner, as they pulled up. Brenda was leaning against her minivan in a pair of velvet black leggings that tied like ribbons around her ankles and a white sports bra, her dark skin already shiny with the oil she liked to apply to make the photos a little more dynamic. A few other people from the studio were hanging out down by the water, all dressed in the same neutral color scheme as Jo had requested. With the lake and greenery in the background, she figured avoiding patterns and vivid colors would be the way to go, and luckily, today was the perfect day for the shoot. The sun glittered off the clear, blue water and rained gently through the canopy of trees. They'd even sent a team to clean up the sand beforehand, making sure there wasn't any trash or rocks in the shots.

Jo quickly listed off the names of everyone here today to Gracie as she pulled into a spot at the end, and gave her shoulder what she hoped was a comforting squeeze before she climbed out of the car.

"Hey, Brenda!" Jo called and slung her camera bag over her shoulder. "Hope you don't mind that I brought an assistant. This is Gracie." Jo turned as she said her name and realized Gracie still hadn't gotten out of the car. Slowly, the girl untangled herself from the seatbelt and joined Jo in the sand.

Brenda met them halfway and held out a hand. "Nice to meet you, Gracie. Are you familiar with yoga?"

"A little." Gracie shrugged. "I used to go to some classes back home with my mom."

"Freshman," Jo clarified.

Brenda nodded, her warm smile never faltering. "Well, feel free to jump into any of the shots if you'd like. You'll fit right in." She gestured toward Gracie's outfit, which did, indeed, match the color scheme—plain black leggings and a cream-colored sweatshirt.

"Wow," said Jo. "Two minutes here and you're already trying to steal my assistant."

Brenda laughed and waved the others over, her long braids whipping around her shoulders as she moved. "Where do you want us first?"

Jo pointed to a spot between the water and the trees, then sank onto one knee and peered into the camera to test the frame. She looked up at Gracie with one eye. "You want to help them with their poses?"

Gracie quickly waved a hand in front of her face. "Oh, I wouldn't know—"

"That's okay!" Jo insisted. "I'll correct it when you're done, but give it a shot. Here, look from where I am, and trust your instincts. What do you think would look good based on what you've gone over in class so far?"

Gracie shot an uncertain look at the group, but without complaint, she walked over to them and started pointing around. Brenda took her spot at the front of the shot in some kind of backbend, and Gracie helped the others fan out around her. Jo slowly lowered the camera, watching as Gracie helped them each into a different pose of varying heights, making perfect levels for the photo while still making sure everyone could be seen. When she turned to head back toward Jo, she kept her eyes trained on the sand.

"Feel free to change whatever—"

Jo grinned. "Gracie, this is great. Let me get a few really quick." Jo sank back into position and fired off a few shots before venturing a little closer. Once she was satisfied she had at least one good one, she waved Gracie back over and held out her camera. "You want to try?"

Gracie's eyes bulged. "I don't—"

"I already got a good shot. Go ahead, try it."

"Hurry!" laughed one of the girls toward the back who was up in a handstand. "My arms are shaking!"

Gracie dropped down into a crouch beside Jo and took the camera with trembling hands.

"Don't worry about it being good," said Jo. "Just do

your thing. Then I can take a look at it and give you some pointers later if you want."

Jo stepped back, giving Gracie some space as she repositioned the camera. "Can you..." Gracie glanced up, squinted, and pointed to one of the girls in the back. "Could you move just a little to your right?"

The girl sank back into a lunge as Gracie fired off her last couple of shots, rose to her feet, and handed the camera back to Jo.

"You guys can relax!" Jo called out, and a chorus relief sounded as everyone unfurled from their poses. She squinted down at the view finder, the corners of her lips curling as she scrolled through Gracie's pictures.

"You can be honest if they're really bad." Gracie hugged her arms to herself.

"Gracie, these look amazing." Jo looked up and grinned at her. "I'm gonna have to force you to be my assistant more often. I might even have to give you some of my pay if I end up using one of these." Jo turned back to the group and waved an arm toward the water. "Can I get three people over here?" Then, over her shoulder she added, "Can you keep an eye on the time? I want to make sure we have enough time to get some good shots at the studio, too, so we don't want to be here longer than an hour."

Gracie nodded and followed Jo as she drifted closer to the water and instructed everyone where to stand. The water lapped against the beach, creating the perfect shot if timed well enough to get the water just over the models' feet.

As they cycled through locations and poses, after Jo was

sure she got at least one good shot, she stepped aside and let Gracie try. After the third round of this, Gracie stepped up without being asked, her hands steady as she took the camera. Jo swapped out her lens halfway through and did some single shots with Brenda in a variety of different poses, then they split off in their separate cars to reconvene at the studio just down the road.

Jo tied up her hair into a ponytail as she climbed into Gracie's car and blew the air out of her cheeks. She was covered in a fine layer of sweat from standing in the sun for an hour, and cursed herself for forgetting sunscreen. Now she was going to look all crispy at the showcase tonight. Yet another thing for her parents to bitch about.

Most likely right after they inquired for the millionth time if she was dating anyone yet.

As if she could read Jo's mind, Gracie asked, "Are you excited for the showcase?"

Jo shrugged and dug around in her bag for her water bottle. "Yes and no. It'll be great for networking, but my parents are flying in. And they're a buzzkill, to say the least. Hopefully Mill and I will be able to come up with an excuse to ditch them afterwards."

Gracie shifted in her seat, her eyes flickering toward Jo as they pulled up to the studio.

"So are you and Miller, like, together?"

Jo nearly choked on her water. "Oh, God, no. We've just been friends since freshman year."

"Oh." A light blush crept up Gracie's neck, and she scratched at the back of her head before turning off the car. "You guys just seem really close."

"Best friends." Jo shrugged and snapped the cap back on her water bottle. "That's what happens when you see each other through all of the different awkward college phases."

"Oh, yeah, I bet." Gracie cleared her throat as she hopped out of the car. "Do you know if he—is he seeing someone else then?"

"You have a thing for Miller?" Jo blurted.

The blush on Gracie's neck intensified and spread all the way up her cheeks. "I just—he's—well, he's really cute, I guess, and—"

"Sorry, sorry. I'm not trying to give you a hard time. No, he's not dating anyone. Do you want me to, uh, talk to him for you or something?"

Gracie's eyes flew wide. "*No*, no! Sorry—just—forget I said anything."

Jo tucked her hands in her pockets and rocked back on her heels. "Already forgotten."

"Cool."

"Cool."

Brenda's car rounded the corner, and Jo let out a deep exhale, her shoulders suddenly tense. She shook it off as the others arrived and they all headed into the studio. It was a beautiful building with intricate woodwork and an entire back wall of floor-to-ceiling windows. It was the kind of place that actually had the potential to convince Jo to try yoga, but she already knew she didn't have enough *zen* in her body for that. Or patience, for that matter.

Gracie was quiet for the rest of the shoot, even once they finished with the models and went around to take pictures of the building. Jo struggled to think of a way to lighten the mood again. She'd been doing so well—Gracie had even seemed to come out of her shell and enjoy herself for a minute there. Jo hadn't meant to embarrass her, and she supposed she shouldn't have been caught that off guard. Plenty of the girls on the paper had a crush on Miller. Jo was willing to bet that was at least half the reason why they'd managed to grow their staff so much. And Gracie seemed nice. The last girl Miller had dated ended up being a nightmare, so maybe someone like Gracie would be good for him.

"Thanks for all of your help today," Jo said as they headed back to the car.

"Thanks for letting me shadow you." Gracie wrung her hands in her lap as Jo pulled up the directions to get back to school.

"Do you have any other questions you need answered? Or you could always email me after if you forgot anything."

"Yeah, I'll have to look over the assignment again, but I'll email you if I need anything else. This was super helpful, so thank you."

A text flashed on Jo's phone as they drove, and she suppressed the urge to groan at the sight of her mom's number. Their flight had just landed, and they wanted to go grab dinner before the showcase. Jo punched in a quick reply, saying she was busy getting ready for the showcase, but maybe they could do it tomorrow night.

Jo checked the time as Gracie pulled up outside her apartment and grimaced. She had less than two hours left to go through the pictures *and* get herself ready. At least her portfolio was digital so she didn't have to worry about getting prints. She would like to edit the pictures at least a little bit, though.

"Thanks again, Gracie," Jo said as she jumped out onto the sidewalk. She froze before closing the door. "Oh! Do you want to give me your number?"

Gracie stared at her for a second, seemingly stunned, before spouting it off. Jo sent her a quick *thank you* text so she'd have her number too and smiled. "See you around!" Then she sprinted up toward the building, her camera bag slapping against her side as she went.

❧ 7 ❧

FRESHMAN YEAR - OCTOBER

A FLASH OF PAIN SPARKED UP JO'S SHOULDER AS SHE twisted her arm behind her back. She hissed through her teeth, and with one final yank, she pulled the zipper the rest of the way up. The dress was a loan from Addie—strapless, floral, and flared out just above the knees. Something that would *never* see the light of day in Jo's closet. But when Jo had gone into their suite's shared bathroom to curl her hair in her original date outfit—black skinny jeans and a maroon crop top—Addie and Liv had gasped in horror and quickly rifled through their closets until they found something more suitable. Jo frowned at herself in the mirror, barely recognizing herself. It wasn't too late to change back—

Someone knocked on her open door. She jumped and whipped around, sighing at the sight of Kayleigh leaning in the doorway in skinny jeans and a black tank top, her hair tied back in a low bun. Jo hadn't even heard her come in.

Kayleigh's eyes swept over Jo's outfit. "You're awfully dressed up. Do I need to change?"

Jo stared at her blankly.

Kayleigh narrowed her eyes, her jaw setting off to the side. "You forgot, didn't you?"

A car honked outside the building, and Jo's eyes darted from Kayleigh to the window. She grimaced, turned, and shoved her belongings in her purse on the desk. "I'm sorry! I have a date with Grey." She leaned forward to check her lip gloss in the mirror one last time.

Kayleigh rolled her eyes so hard, her whole head banged back against the door. "Of course," she muttered.

"Kayleigh, I'm sorry—"

"You were supposed to help me pick out a dress for my lacrosse induction ceremony, remember? It's *tomorrow*. I have to get the dress today."

Jo froze with one finger on her lips. *Shit.*

And Grey was already outside.

It was too late to cancel.

Her eyes widened as an idea formed, and she jabbed her thumb toward their shared wall. "Maybe Addie or Liv—"

"Oh, please." Kayleigh spun on her heel and headed for the door.

"Kayleigh..." Jo's phone dinged with a text from Grey, letting her know he was here. "I totally forgot. I really am sorry."

Kayleigh paused in front of the door, her back still to Jo. "You know, this is the third time in a row you've canceled on me for him."

That couldn't be right. Surely it had only been once,

maybe twice... "Kayleigh—" Her phone buzzed again, and she glanced down.

Kayleigh let out another impatient huff. "Just don't be surprised if none of us are left when things don't work out." And with that, she disappeared into the hallway and slammed the door behind her.

THE ENTIRE CAMPUS HAD TRANSFORMED WITH THE TURN of the season, and a crown of multicolored trees framed Grey from behind. Golden leaves crunched underfoot as Jo made her way toward him. He'd ditched the black-T-shirt-and-leather-jacket ensemble for a burgundy sweater and jeans today, his gold-framed sunglasses hanging from the neckline. His black Volvo sat on the curb behind him.

A corner of Grey's mouth lifted as he opened the passenger door for her. He circled the car and slid into the seat beside her. "Mind if we take the scenic route?"

"Scenic route?" Jo asked.

He spun the steering wheel to maneuver them out of the parking lot, the half-smile still on his face. "I'm taking that as a yes." He headed in the opposite direction of the highway, the radio playing lowly in the background. Jo leaned her head against the door to look out the window as they wound along the curving backroads, lush trees of vibrant red and gold framing them on either side. Most of the houses were fully decked out in Halloween décor—spiderwebs, scarecrows, skeletons who looked like they were scaling the side of the house.

Grey's warm hand slid into her lap, his fingers gently pressing into the skin above her knee. Her body flooded with heat at the contact, but still, in the very back of her mind, in a voice barely louder than a whisper, the words *when things don't work out* played over and over again.

Not *if*.

When.

The thoughts lingered in her mind long into the afternoon, even once they made it downtown and wove through the sea of food trucks, colorful umbrellas, and bustling crowds. They stopped at one of the picnic benches beneath the rows of string lights after Grey grabbed two hot ciders. They sat in silence for a few minutes, just watching the people around them, until he nudged her foot under the table.

"What's going on with you?" he asked. "You shut down."

"Sorry." Jo twisted the cup around in her hands. "I had a fight with my roommate right before I left, and I feel really bad about it."

He tilted his head to the side. "What was the fight about?"

Jo sipped her drink and glanced back at the snaking line to the nearby candy apple truck. "I've been canceling a lot on her lately—more than I realized. And today it was something important, and I just completely forgot. Which is shitty. Really shitty. And she's pissed."

He leaned back in his seat. "You had plans with her today? You should've told me. We could've done this another time."

Jo shrugged. "I didn't find out until you were already outside."

Grey paused, his mouth setting to the side as he considered this. "What were the plans?"

"I was supposed to help her pick out a dress for this thing."

"Down here?" He gestured around them.

Jo nodded, and he flapped his hand, gesturing to her phone on the table. "Then tell her to come meet us, and we'll both help her find something."

A slow smile crept onto Jo's face. "You want to help my roommate pick out a dress?"

"I want to be the knight in shining armor who mends the relationship between you and your roommate so I can hold it over you forever," he said matter-of-factly.

Jo snorted, but picked up her phone. "Of course." She paused. "Would you really not mind?"

"Stop stalling. Here, I'll call her." He pulled the phone out of her hands and started scrolling through her contacts. "What's her name?"

Jo set her cup back on the table and covered her face with her hands. "Kayleigh."

"Aha." Grey held the phone up to his ear and winked. "Hello, Kayleigh. Sorry, this is Grey. I believe I intruded on your plans today. So I'd like to propose you come join Johanna and me downtown. No, really, it wouldn't be any trouble."

There was silence on the other end of the phone for several seconds. Grey drummed his fingers on the table and shrugged. Jo couldn't make out whatever she said next, but judging by the grin that appeared on Grey's face, it was a *yes*.

"Perfect. I'll send you our location. We're right over by the food trucks. Great. We'll wait here for you. See you soon." He hung up the phone and handed it back to her.

Jo narrowed her eyes but couldn't quite hide her smile as she took the phone. "Do you have any idea what you just got yourself into?" she asked.

He shrugged, reached across the table, and slid his fingers through hers. "Just doing my part for the good of society. Saving the world one roommate relationship at a time."

Jo wasn't sure if Kayleigh really couldn't decide on a dress, or if she was making a point and trying to punish Jo for canceling on her so many times. Either way, Jo bit her tongue as Kayleigh carted yet another mountain of options back to the dressing room. Jo's feet were starting to ache from standing so long. Grey chuckled lightly, his lips brushing the back of her ear as he trailed his knuckles over her shoulder and down her arm. She leaned back into his chest and sighed.

"If you decided to sneak out the back door and leave me here, I wouldn't blame you," she said.

He locked his arms around her shoulders and rested his chin on the top of her head. "How much do you want to bet she ends up picking that first one she tried on?"

"I'm sorry." She turned around to face him. "I know this isn't exactly what you had in mind for today."

"Why are you apologizing? I'm the one who suggested it." He wrapped his arms back around her shoulders and pulled her against his chest. "How about you and I go for a drive once she finishes up here? At this rate, we might catch the sunset."

Jo snorted. Their date had started at *noon*. "I'd like that."

"Okay!" The curtains to the dressing room flew open with a grand *whoosh*. Kayleigh stepped out with a shimmery white dress in hand—*the* shimmery white dress she'd tried on an hour and a half ago. "I think I found the winner."

"Pay up," murmured Grey.

Kayleigh's nose scrunched up at the sight of the two of them tangled together. "You two should just go get a room or something already. I can handle this from here."

Jo supposed that was as close to a *thank you* as she was going to get. She detached herself from Grey and went to give Kayleigh a hug. "I'm glad you found something you liked," she said.

Kayleigh huffed a bit, but returned the hug. "I'll see you back at the room?" she asked.

Jo nodded.

The sun actually *was* starting to set as they made it back to Grey's car. Instead of heading back to Jo's dorm, he went the opposite direction, toward the coast. Jo propped her arms on the car door and rested her chin against them, her gaze trained out the window. The lights of the city faded behind them, giving way to a sea of lush, green trees and bright red leaves. Shades of pink, blue, and yellow rippled along the clouds lingering in the sky, the colors reflecting off the asphalt, still slightly damp from the rain earlier. A rock song on the radio played in the background, and Grey hummed along, drumming his fingers absently against the steering wheel as they followed the curving road out of the city.

"What are you thinking about?" he murmured.

Jo leaned her head to the side and smiled. "That I wish I had my camera."

"We'll make a special trip for that next time."

"Oh, next time, huh?"

"I'm still on a trial period?" He brought his hand to his chest and shook his head. "I'm hurt, Jo."

She snorted. "No you're not."

"No I'm not on a trial period, or no I'm not hurt?"

She propped her feet on the dashboard and leaned back in her seat. "Doesn't it ever get exhausting?"

His eyes flickered away from the road to look at her, just for a moment. "What does?"

She waved her hand in his general direction. "Trying to be funny."

He laughed as he turned back to the road. "I don't know if I should be offended or not. You realize you're in my car, right? I could kick you out at any moment."

"You won't."

"And why is that?"

She shrugged. "You like me too much."

She expected him to laugh again, but he just reached

over, his hand finding hers. "That I do, Johanna. That I do."

KAYLEIGH WAS WEARING THE DRESS WHEN JO STEPPED back into the dorm, twirling around, a different shoe on each foot. Pink tinged her cheeks when she spotted Jo standing in the mirror behind her. "I can't decide on the shoes," she explained, lifting the skirt a little higher, revealing a simple nude pump on one foot and a strappy black stiletto on the other.

Jo gestured to the black ones. "Those are more fun."

"That's what I was thinking." Kayleigh leaned down to undo the clasp and grinned up at Jo through her hair. "How'd it go with Grey?"

"Oh, you know," said Jo breezily as she collapsed onto her bed.

"You know, I thought he'd end up being a douche. But I actually kind of like him."

Jo snorted. "Gee, thanks."

"That's the best compliment that roommate stealer is going to get from me." She paused, then added, her voice a little quieter, "I'm sorry about what I said earlier."

Jo rolled her head to look at her as Kayleigh shimmied out of the dress, draped it carefully over the back of her wardrobe door, and slipped on some sweats. "Well, you've got me for the rest of the night. Wanna get drunk and watch trashy TV?"

Kayleigh's eyes widened. "Wanna go get chicken nuggets first?"

Jo closed her eyes and threw her head back against the bed. "Yesssss."

After grabbing shoes and bags in a flurry of movement, they hurried out of the suite, passing Liv and Addie doing their makeup in the common area.

"Where are you two going?" asked Liv.

"Sorry!" Kayleigh grabbed Jo's hand and pulled her into the hallway. "Roommates only!"

Jo burst into giggles as they tripped over each other, landing in a tangle of limbs together on the floor. The door across the hall opened, and Miller's head popped out. He took in Kayleigh and Jo laying on top of each other and smirked.

"Carry on." He nodded and slipped back into his room.

"We should get those fried macaroni bites too," Kayleigh whispered.

"Maybe some tots," Jo added.

"Milkshakes?" said Kayleigh.

Jo nodded vigorously. "Definitely milkshakes."

Kayleigh's hand tightened around Jo's. "If we hurry, we might be able to get that happy hour deal."

Jo sprang up from the floor, dragging Kayleigh along behind her. "My car is in the lot out back!"

Kayleigh immediately took over the radio as they slid into Jo's Jeep and hurried down the road, her car dinging in protest until they both put their seatbelts on.

"Are we thinking throwbacks?" asked Kayleigh.

"Definitely."

The drive-through line was nearly wrapped all the way around the restaurant when they pulled up, and Jo's eyes flickered to the clock. Just ten minutes left before their happy hour ended.

"I think we'll make it," said Kayleigh, leaning back in her seat and propping her feet on the dash. The brake lights in front of them cast a red tint to her skin. When she turned to look at Jo again, a mischievous smile had crept onto her face. "So are you going to share any of the juicy details about Grey, or am I going to have to pull them out of you?"

Jo rolled her eyes and crept the car forward. "Maybe there aren't any juicy details."

"With a guy that hot? There absolutely must be. Is he a good kisser?"

Heat crept up the back of Jo's neck as a few choice memories rose up in her mind—Grey's hands expertly gliding up her shirt, his tongue sweeping into her mouth, his body tightening against hers. She coughed. "Yeah. Yeah, he is."

Kayleigh snorted out a laugh and pointed at Jo's face. "Damn, I wish I had a guy to kiss me so good that I looked like that. Have you guys had the awkward *what are we* talk yet?"

Jo tightened her hands around the steering wheel and grimaced. "No. But we're not even hooking up yet, so like it can't be just *that*..." She glanced at Kayleigh sideways. "Right?"

Kayleigh shrugged. "Don't look at me. Though, if he

was just trying to get into your pants, the guy is putting in a *lot* of work, so I doubt it. He seems really into you."

"Do you think it's weird that we haven't talked about it yet?"

Kayleigh paused, considering this. "How long have you guys been seeing each other?"

Jo grimaced again. "Like two months."

Kayleigh scrunched her nose. "Maybe you should just, like, casually bring it up. Make it a joke, you know? Maybe he's just assumed you guys were already."

"Yeah, maybe," echoed Jo as she pulled up to the speaker. She checked her phone as she rolled down her window and waited for the person to take her order. There was a text from Grey from around the time he'd dropped her off. Her stomach fluttered the way it always did at the sight of his name on her phone.

Today was fun. When can I see you again?

A small smile crept onto her face.

The speaker crackled outside her window, and Kayleigh immediately leaned across the seat and called out, "Yeah, we'll take one of everything!"

❦ 8 ❦

SENIOR YEAR - MARCH

JO SHOWED UP TO THE SHOWCASE FIVE MINUTES BEFORE the doors opened to the public with partially wet hair and hastily scrawled eyeliner. But her photos were now perfectly edited and uploaded to her portfolio, and that was all that mattered. She'd shimmied her way into a sleek, black dress that cut off mid-thigh. The neckline slashed across her chest, the thin straps overlapping on a single shoulder. She'd gone with her basic black heels that were comfortable enough to stand in all night and pumped enough product in her hair that hopefully it would still look decent once it finished air-drying.

The theater's lobby was packed with rows of tables, sectioned off for each senior's display. She hurried over to her spot at the end of the first row and turned on her monitor. The first page of her portfolio flickered into view, and she quickly dusted off the surrounding table and laid out her business cards along the shimmery gold decorations she'd picked up that morning.

The boy next to her had a massive poster board set up like this was some kind of science fair. Samples of his multimedia work were spread out across his station. Jo wasn't sure exactly what he did, but from a brief glance, it looked like a combination between photography, newspaper papier-mâché, and something that looked like concrete. Jo craned her neck, looking for Miller, but couldn't make him out among the rows of heads and projects. She was pretty sure the people who were just here for their minors had been placed in the back.

Sucking in a deep breath, she smoothed her hands over her dress. She wasn't sure what she was more anxious about, seeing her parents or Sandra Simone—if Sandra even came by her booth. Maybe that would be worse, to know her idol had been in this very room but hadn't gotten the opportunity to see Jo's work.

Jo pressed play on her monitor so her portfolio would constantly be revolving across the screen. She busied herself by sweeping the room, taking in the other seniors' projects as best she could from her vantage point, hoping if she kept her brain distracted enough, there wouldn't be enough room left for nerves.

At first when the doors opened, the guests just barely trickled in. After about fifteen minutes, more people arrived, and the room came to life, buzzing with conversations and movement, the narrow aisles between booths filling with bodies. Several people stopped by Jo's station and took her business cards, complimenting her work and asking about her post-grad plans. Some left their own business cards, saying they'd be in touch. She smiled politely and forced herself not to fidget or look around the room, but the anxiety was a constant presence, like static on her skin, as she desperately waited for the right person to appear.

Jo didn't recognize her at first. She was in a sleek red dress, her dark hair twisted into an intricate bun on the top of her head, and bold, gold hoops dangled from her ears. She gave a small smile and nodded as she stepped in front of Jo's screen and watched as the pictures cycled through. She didn't say anything, not until the very last picture flashed across the screen and the montage started again.

"I'm Sandra Simone," the woman finally said.

"I know," Jo said without thinking. "I mean—I'm a big fan of your work."

That same small smile crossed Sandra Simone's face as she leaned forward and gingerly picked up one of Jo's business cards. The paper suddenly looked flimsy and unprofessional now that it was between her perfectly manicured fingernails. "Are you free tomorrow, Johanna?" she asked.

Jo hesitated a moment too long before stuttering out, "Yes, I'm free."

The woman gave a single, satisfied nod. "Good. Come in for an interview at my office. Two o'clock."

Jo stared at her in shock, but forced herself to respond. "Absolutely."

And with that, Sandra Simone laid her own business card on Jo's table, turned, and disappeared back into the crowd. Jo's heart continued to thunder against her ribs long after she was gone, and she steadied herself back against the table with trembling hands. She felt like she needed someone to pinch her. Hell, she needed someone to *punch* her.

"Hey, Jo!" A face swam into view—red cheeks, nervous smile. Gracie. She hesitated a few feet away from Jo's booth in a lacy white dress and matching sneakers, awkwardly shifting her weight back and forth.

"Gracie?" Jo's voice rose into a question, but she quickly masked it with a smile and waved the girl over. "What are you doing here willingly? Did Sanders offer extra credit or something for showing up?"

"No." She shifted again, her eyes darting from the portfolio on the screen to the business cards to Jo's face. "I just...wanted to stop by and say hi, I guess. And see how your portfolio turned out. Did you add any of the yoga ones?"

"Yes!" Jo grabbed the remote and quickly shuffled to the new additions, her chest warming at Gracie's words. She barely knew Jo, but she'd still come by to support her. "Here they are." She landed on a shot of three people by the lake, the sun reflecting off the water just so.

Gracie leaned in, tilting her head to the side as she examined it. "Oh my God. It looks even better than I thought. Do you think you could show me how you edited it like this?"

Jo smiled. "Anytime."

Gracie's gaze landed somewhere behind Jo's head. Her cheeks immediately turned scarlet, and she dropped her gaze back to the floor. Jo pressed her lips together to keep her smirk in. At least she knew where Miller's booth was now.

"Thanks for stopping by." Jo squeezed Gracie's shoulder. "You should wander around! I'm sure some people have way more impressive stuff than mine."

"I doubt it." Gracie offered a small wave as she shuffled around the corner. Jo smirked as she watched her little blonde head disappear into the next row of booths. There was something eerily familiar about Gracie, something she couldn't quite place. Obviously, she'd been on the newspaper staff all year, but it was something more than that.

She reminded her of Meredith, Jo realized. Her best friend from back home.

"Johanna!"

Her head snapped up at the familiar voice, the smile immediately falling from her face. Her parents pushed through the crowd in perfectly coordinated outfits—her father in a navy blue suit, her mother in a white dress with navy accents. Her mom pulled her into a hug, momentarily drowning Jo in her perfume. Her hair was pulled back and styled the way she usually wore it to work—honestly, Jo was half surprised she wasn't wearing her flight attendant uniform. Her dad pulled her into a side hug next and leaned over to squint at her portfolio, his ever-present pilot's pin front and center on his suit jacket.

"These are really good, Johanna!"

She ignored the surprise in his voice as he moved on to inspect her business cards on the table. Her mother picked up a strand of her wet hair between two fingers, but mercifully, she didn't say anything.

"You'll never believe who just stopped by," Jo said under her breath, her eyes flicking over their shoulders to make sure Sandra wasn't nearby to hear.

"Who?" asked her father.

"*Sandra Simone*—I know you probably don't know who that is. But she's this amazing, award-winning photographer, and she asked me to come in for an interview tomorrow."

Her dad grinned. "That's my girl. So we'll go out to dinner tomorrow night to celebrate!"

"Are you seeing anyone?" her mother asked. "Because if you are, you should bring him to dinner. I'd love to meet him."

Jo tried not to let her irritation show. Here she was all excited about an amazing career opportunity, and all her mom wanted to talk about was boys.

"No," Jo said flatly.

Her mom pursed her lips, her eyes drifting to the boy at the booth beside them. She gave him a quick once-over, clearly deeming him not suitable. "You know," she continued, as her eyes moved on to scan the rest of the room's prospects. "Once you're out of college, it'll be even harder to meet men." She lowered her voice at the end as if *men* were a dirty word. "If you don't find a boyfriend now, it'll just be harder for you in the long run. And you're not getting any younger. And you're so beautiful—don't let that go to waste."

"Mom," Jo warned.

Her mom shrugged innocently and glanced from Jo to

her husband. "I don't think it's unreasonable for your mother to worry about your future happiness."

"Anyway." Jo cleared her throat. "What do you think of my portfolio? I'm still hoping to add a few more shots before I graduate."

"Your pictures have always been good, Johanna, we know that," her mother said, apparently exasperated by the subject, and Jo glanced around the room for an out. She met Miller's gaze across the room and widened her eyes in a desperate *help me* plea before turning back to her parents. She didn't want to have this conversation—not ever, but especially not now. But she was trapped at her station, and mortifyingly, judging by the amused curve of the lips of the boy beside her, he was overhearing everything.

"Have you thought of online dating?" her mother continued. "I know it's not ideal, but apparently it's what all of the kids are doing these days—"

"*There* you are." Someone appeared on Jo's right, but she didn't have a chance to look before his head swerved around and pressed his lips to hers. She froze, momentarily stunned, but then a wave of his scent rushed over her.

Miller.

His lips lingered on hers for a beat, his warm hand cupping the side of her face. Heat slowly crept down her spine as she leaned into him and pressed a single hand against his chest. When he pulled away, he hesitated a few inches from her face, eyes locking with hers in a silent question. She nodded slightly as he pulled back the rest of the way and faced her parents, feigning surprise at their presence.

"I'm so sorry. I'm Miller, Jo's boyfriend." He extended his hand to her mother first, who was beaming so wide, she looked like she might explode. Her father, on the other hand, looked less than pleased, but he shook Miller's hand when he offered it. "Have you had a chance to look at Jo's portfolio yet?" Miller asked. "It's the best one here by far."

Her father's expression softened at that, and he glanced around the rest of the lobby. "Is one of these yours?" he asked.

Miller ducked his head and pointed toward the back. "We're not technically supposed to abandon our posts, but that's mine over there. Graphic design is only my minor, so this is more of a formality for me than a networking thing like it is for Jo."

"What's your major then?" Jo's dad asked.

"I'm a double major—English Lit and Criminal Justice."

Jo's father raised his eyebrows—apparently this was an acceptable answer. Jo's mom looked about ready to swoon.

"Anyway, I should get back over there before one of the professors sees me, but it was nice to meet you both."

"You should come to dinner with us tomorrow!" Jo's mom insisted. "After Jo's interview."

Miller turned to her. "Interview?"

She shrugged, unable to suppress her grin, and flipped the newly acquired business card around her fingers. "I guess Sandra Simone liked my portfolio."

A grin of his own stretched across his features, and he subtly offered a fist to pound. "I'd do something more extreme, but I won't embarrass you by making a scene. At least not until we leave the building."

THE ANTI-RELATIONSHIP YEAR 103

Jo laughed and pushed him toward his station. "Go back to where you're supposed to be."

He did a small bow, but turned to Jo's mom before leaving. "I'd love to come to dinner." He paused halfway down the row, met Jo's eyes over her parents' heads, and winked.

"Thank you," she mouthed when her parents weren't looking, then braced herself for the flood of questions to follow.

9

FRESHMAN YEAR - OCTOBER

"So have you and Grey done it yet?"

Jo stopped pushing the chicken tenders around on her plate and blinked back to the lunch table in front of her. The roar of the surrounding crowd slowly trickled in, building until her ears buzzed with it. She'd been having a hard time staying present all day, like her brain was refusing to participate in this reality. She didn't even notice her mind wandering or her vision unfocusing until someone drew her back.

Kayleigh stared at her expectantly from across the table. Her mascara was slightly smudged from the rain. Jo shot a quick glance at Miller beside her, but he was thumbing through a book, pointedly *not* listening.

Jo sighed and gathered her hair into a high ponytail. She and Grey had gotten close to having sex plenty of times—every time she was with him, if she were being honest—but every time, she'd pulled away. It wasn't that she didn't want to, exactly. But she didn't know how to tell him it would be her first time, or if she even should. And she couldn't shake off this feeling that the moment they did it, everything would change between them.

"Not yet," she mumbled.

"Isn't he going on tour, like, tomorrow?" asked Kayleigh. "It'll be your last chance for a while."

Jo had been pointedly *not* thinking about that. They'd be gone on tour for months—she wouldn't even see him again until next semester. She wasn't just assuming they'd pick up where they left off—she wasn't that naïve. But still...

"Just leave her alone," muttered Miller.

"If the sex talk bothers you, go sit with the boys!" Kayleigh pointed across the room to where Foster and Gatsby were sitting with the other fraternity pledges. It looked like they were piling as many condiments on a plate as possible and chanting until one of them ate a spoonful.

Miller flipped the page. "I'd rather be around people with more than one brain cell, thanks."

"So are you going to see him tonight?" asked Kayleigh.

Jo nodded. "I'm going over to his place to hang out."

Kayleigh *ooooohed.*

"Not like that." Jo rolled her eyes. "Other people will be there too. It's like a going-away party."

Miller brought his hand to his chest. "And we weren't invited?"

Jo raised her eyebrows. "Do you want to come?"

"Not if you're going to be banging Grey in the bathroom!" shrilled Kayleigh, loud enough that the table next to them all turned around to look. Jo stared them down until they looked away.

"No, really," said Jo. "You guys should come. You haven't really gotten to know Grey yet anyway—we can do a pregame and everything."

"I'm in," said Kayleigh. "I've been *waiting* for you to introduce me to his hot band friends."

"Miller?" Jo kicked him under the table. "Tell me you'll come."

He closed his book with an audible *thunk*. "Fine. But you'll have to get me really drunk first."

GREY'S APARTMENT WAS ON THE TWENTIETH FLOOR OF A high-rise downtown. Despite the hundreds of windows littering the side of the building, Jo had come to recognize exactly which one was his from the street. Today it was full of life, the shades wide open, red lights flashing inside. Car horns blared as their Uber pulled to the side of the street.

Jo stumbled out first and righted her plaid skirt as Kayleigh and Miller climbed out after her. They were both in jeans, making Jo feel a little out of place next to them in her mesh top and high heels, but Grey liked when she wore skirts. And this was the last night she'd see him for months —something she had to force herself to stop thinking about. She teetered a bit on the sidewalk, the vodka hitting her harder than usual since she'd skipped dinner. It hadn't been intentional. She hadn't been able to muster an appetite since that conversation at lunch.

The doorman nodded as they headed inside and quietly shuffled toward the elevator, trying not to draw any attention. Judging by the stiff set of Miller's shoulders and the way Kayleigh was practically holding on to him for dear life as they crossed the lobby, Jo wasn't the only one affected by the pregame.

Jo led them down Grey's floor, though the apartment would've been easy to find regardless from the music spilling into the hallway. It doubled in volume as someone swung the door open.

"Oh. It's you." Lisa, United Fates' drummer, stood in the doorway, her hair in two long braids. She looked Jo's companions up and down, her eyes slightly squinted, as if calculating something.

"Is Grey here?" Jo finally asked when Lisa didn't step aside to let them in.

"Grey!" Lisa called over her shoulder. "*Johanna's* here."

Jo stiffened, not quite sure what to make of the tone Lisa used when she said her name, but she knew she didn't like it. A million little doubts fluttered in the back of her mind, urging her to turn around and leave. Maybe he didn't want her here.

Maybe she was just making a fool of herself.

She felt a warm hand on her back.

"Johanna!" Grey appeared in the doorway, hair sticking straight up, a dark gray T-shirt rumpled and half tucked into his black jeans. "So glad you could make it. And you brought friends! Wait—you two were at the concert!"

"Kayleigh and Miller," said Jo.

Grey nodded and flashed what seemed like a genuine

smile. "Welcome! Come on in. We've got drinks in the kitchen. And we *had* snacks in the living room."

Heads turned in their direction as they entered, though there were fewer people there than Jo had expected, no more than a dozen. She followed Grey to the kitchen and gratefully accepted a red plastic cup, tipping the contents back without even asking what was in it. She glanced through the cutout above the kitchen island that showed into the living room. Every seat on the couch was occupied, and the room reeked of weed. An ashtray and a few empty chip bowls littered the coffee table.

Arms snaked around Johanna's waist and pulled her against a warm chest. Grey's scent enveloped her as he pressed a kiss to the top of her head. Kayleigh and Miller lingered in the kitchen door, sipping from their cups and eyeing the crowd in the living room. The contrast between Grey's friends and hers was more stark than she'd realized. She'd been expecting a lot more people to be here as a buffer, but now she was thinking maybe inviting Kayleigh and Miller hadn't been smart.

Another wave of weed hit Jo, and she turned around to see smoke filling the living room.

"Would you at least open the window?" called Grey. He gave Jo a small squeeze before letting her go and heading to the opposite wall to open the balcony door.

Jo turned to Kayleigh and Miller and grimaced. "Is this okay? I'm sorry, I thought there would be more people here."

"Would you hate us if we, like, went to a coffee shop down the street or something? We'll wait as long as you

want to stay so we can head back together but..."
Kayleigh wrapped her arms around herself and pursed her lips.

But she didn't want to be here.

"No, yeah, that's totally fine." Jo nodded a few too many times, though a sudden fist of panic squeezed her chest at the thought of them leaving.

"I think I saw a diner down the street," Miller offered.

Jo bit her lip and glanced over at Grey. He was still by the balcony door and grinned when he caught her eye, nodding for her to join him.

"You stay," Kayleigh insisted. "It's your last night with him. And just text us when you want to go home, okay?"

Miller shifted on his feet, his gaze darting between Jo and Kayleigh. "Unless you don't want us to leave," he added. "I don't want to leave you alone here."

"She's not alone. She's with Grey," said Kayleigh.

This didn't seem to make Miller feel better in the slightest.

"You guys go," said Jo, putting as much certainty in her words as she could muster. "I'll text you later."

No one in the living room so much as looked up as Kayleigh and Miller headed out, nor did they glance at Jo as she squeezed through them to get to Grey on the other side.

"Come on." He took her hand and led her onto the balcony. It had a great view of the city, especially at night when the lights made everything glow, but the balcony itself was little more than a narrow slab of concrete with two lawn chairs shoved in the corner. Grey sank into one of them and pulled Jo onto his lap. If he'd noticed Miller and Kayleigh leaving, he didn't mention it.

"Sorry about all of them in there," he murmured instead, his lips resting against her bare shoulder. "They're friends of Pete's, mostly. And they're leaving in a bit to head to a club around the corner."

"You're not going with them?" Jo asked. "Isn't this supposed to be your going-away party?"

His hands slid around her waist, and he rested his palms flat against her stomach. "Staying here with you seems like much more fun."

She shifted on his lap. Despite the chairs being nestled far enough back in the shadows that no one inside could see them, she was still very much aware of their presence. It was hard not to be with the pulsing music, roaring laughter, and the stench of weed in the air so strong she could feel a coating of it on her tongue. The alcohol burned through her, leaving her limbs loose and light. She sipped whatever was in the red cup, barely able to taste it anymore. Grey traced his fingers along her forearm, the touch featherlight. His chin rested in the small space between her neck and shoulder, scratching the delicate skin there with the stubble on his jaw. They'd been seeing each other for only a few months—logically, Jo knew this—but still, it had become so easy, him and her. This stance. The familiarity of his smell, the way his skin felt against hers. The certainty that she would hear from him each morning. The rush of serotonin every time his name appeared on her phone.

She wasn't sure if she was ready to lose it.

"What are you thinking about?" he murmured.

"You leaving," she admitted.

His arms tightened around her as his lips brushed the side of her neck. "It's a short tour," he murmured.

"I know." She tried to keep her voice light, unconcerned, but it still quavered a bit at the end.

"Here's an idea." His teeth scraped along the side of her neck. "Just drop out of school and come with us."

She laughed and let her head fall to the side.

His tongue slowly traced along her throat as his hands slid beneath her shirt. She closed her eyes, breathing in the fresh air of the night, focusing on the heat of his hands against the skin of her stomach. Her heart pounded almost painfully hard against her ribs. Then she realized she could hear it because the music was no longer pulsing out onto the balcony.

"Your friends left," she murmured.

"Mm-hmm." He nodded against her neck as his fingers slid her skirt farther up her thighs, high enough that he could easily slide his hand underneath. It wasn't the first time he'd tried this.

But it was the first time she let him.

Suddenly all of her nerves from before, the second-guessing, the overthinking—it all just...stopped. Her skin burned, the heat tingling along every nerve and traveling from her toes to the roots of her hair and back again, in part from the alcohol, and partly from the way he was touching her. He started to slide her sleeve down her shoulder, and she stopped him, laying her hand over his.

"You are *not* undressing me out here," she said.

He chuckled against her back, his lips not even pausing the pattern they were tracing along her neck. "Then by all means, let me take you to my room."

Before she could respond, he swept her into his arms and stood. At first she thought he'd head straight for the balcony door, but instead, he set her on her feet and backed her up until she was pressed against the balcony's railing. His fingers threaded into her hair as his mouth landed on hers, his knee pushing between her legs. There was nothing soft or cautious about this kiss. This was the kiss of a man who knew he was about to get what he wanted.

He kissed Jo like he was making up for every time their time had been cut short over the past month, every time they were interrupted, every time she made them stop. And she let him. She let his hips press her against the railing and his hands slide under her clothes. She let his teeth dig into the skin of her neck until she gasped. She let him lift her by the waist until her legs were wrapped around him and he was carrying her back into the apartment.

She didn't even have a chance to worry if she was doing things right, because he laid her out on the bed and immediately took over, until it became a continuous stream of things she let him do. She let him slip off her skirt, unclasp her bra, kiss any part of her skin he could get his mouth on. He knelt back and peeled off his shirt, and she laid back and watched, like he was the main performer in this routine and she was only an observer. Aside from the city lights pouring in through the window, the room was dark.

As he hovered over her, he laced their hands together and pinned them above her head, and she realized he was breathing just as heavily as she was.

"Are you sure?" he murmured as his lips trailed down the side of her jaw. "You want to do this tonight?"

She nodded, breathless, as one of his hands slid down her body, taking its time, before finally coming between her legs. She closed her eyes, willing herself to relax, willing herself to stop *thinking* so much, and she felt his lips press against hers again, his tongue eagerly sweeping into her mouth.

"Just, can we use a condom?" she breathed.

"Of course." He pulled on the lobe of her ear with his teeth, and when he spoke again, she could hear the smile in his voice. "I've been waiting for this for a long time."

WHEN HE WAS DONE, GREY ROLLED ONTO HIS BACK beside her and let out a deep exhale. Jo continued to stare at the ceiling, her entire body numb. Grey traced his hand down her arm, linked their fingers together, and pulled her against his chest.

It was done. This thing she'd built up in her mind for so long—this insurmountable rite of passage—that was it. Grey kissed her temple and leaned down to meet her gaze, and she forced a smile, willing the spiraling thoughts in her mind to quiet. He opened his mouth to say something, but a buzzing across the room cut him off.

"Hold on." He untangled himself from her and jumped

up to grab his phone off the dresser. While his back was turned, Jo took the opportunity to grab the sheets and wrap them around herself. She wasn't sure why she was doing it—he'd already seen everything—but there was something about this moment afterwards that felt so much more vulnerable.

"Yeah, yeah, I hear you," Grey was saying into the phone. Jo pushed herself up, sheets firmly wrapped around her chest, and leaned back against the headboard. A cold wave of dread washed through her chest, and she quickly glanced down at the sheets around her, but there wasn't any blood, at least not that she could tell. It hadn't hurt—not as much as she'd prepared herself for, at least—but it hadn't felt *good* exactly, either. "I'll be there in a bit."

Grey hung up the phone and turned back to her, grinning as he took her in on the bed. He climbed toward her and placed his hands against the headboard on either side of her face, leaning in until their noses brushed.

"That was the guys," he said. "They're pissed I'm not there. I promised I'd stop by for a bit tonight. Do you mind?"

It took her a few seconds to process what he was saying. He wanted to...leave?

Or rather, he wanted *her* to leave.

Heat flooded to the back of her neck, but she clenched her jaw to keep it from showing on her face. "Of course not. It's getting late, anyway. I should get home."

"Great. Okay." He pressed his lips to her forehead and jumped back up, immediately searching the ground for his pants. "No rush at all. Stay as long as you want."

She watched numbly as he quickly collected his things, checked his hair in the mirror, and headed toward the door, all while Jo was still frozen in place against his headboard. He paused in the doorway to glance back at her, that crooked smile still firmly in place. "You're beautiful, Johanna."

And then he left.

It wasn't until after the door shut behind him that she realized he hadn't even asked her to come with him.

She let out a shuddering breath. When she glanced down, she realized how tightly her hands were clenched around the sheet. The surrounding silence rang in her ears.

She couldn't spend another minute in this apartment.

She leapt up, her breaths coming in short, harsh gasps as she searched the ground for her clothes and yanked them on with trembling hands. Then suddenly every part of her body was shaking, expelling whatever emotion that was pouring into her chest but she couldn't quite recognize. Tears burned at the corners of her eyes, and she had to sit on the edge of the bed for a minute to catch her breath.

She found her phone last, grimacing as she noticed the time. It was a lot later than she'd realized. She quickly pulled up her text conversations with Miller.

Are you guys still there?

His response was immediate.

Still here! Everything okay?

She glanced around the empty apartment, at the rumpled sheets on the bed, the discarded Solo cups on the floor, the pile of dirty clothes in the corner she hadn't noticed before. There was a lacy bra on top that definitely didn't belong to her. A hot tear rolled down her cheek, but she quickly swiped it away.

I'll be there in five.

BY THE TIME SHE MADE IT TO THE DINER, IT WAS EMPTY, save for a single booth in the back. Miller waved as she approached, his legs propped carelessly on the bright red seat across from him.

"Where's Kayleigh?" Jo asked.

"Oh, she went home about an hour ago."

Jo wrapped her arms around herself and glanced at the surrounding empty tables again. "So you've just been in here all by yourself all night?"

He shrugged, like this wasn't a particularly odd thing for him to do, and waved his phone at her. "I've got some books on here to help pass the time. Come on, have a seat." He straightened, letting his feet fall back to the ground.

"Thanks for waiting for me. I know it's late. You didn't have to do that—but, thanks." She wasn't sure what she would've done if he hadn't answered. She slid in across from him, not quite meeting his eyes. Somehow, she knew if he saw her face—really saw it—he'd know everything. But sitting across from him right now felt a hell of a lot better than being alone in that apartment. They sat in silence like that until, finally, Jo looked up.

He stared at her for a second, his expression giving

nothing away. But then he turned and nodded toward the waitress reading a romance novel behind the counter. "You in the mood for some fries? My treat."

She let out a startled laugh, her breath hitching in the middle, so she coughed to disguise it. Of all the things she'd thought he'd say, that wasn't even on the list of possibilities. "You don't have to do that."

He shrugged and waved over the waitress. "It's cool. Next time, it'll be your turn."

10

SENIOR YEAR - MARCH

THE NEXT DAY, MILLER APPEARED AT HER DOOR, CAR keys and a plastic-wrapped sandwich in hand. The moment Jo told him where Sandra's office was, he'd insisted on driving since there was some famous bookstore nearby he wanted to go to. She was supposed to have a therapy appointment that afternoon, which she'd already rescheduled twice, but if there was anything her therapist would agree was worth rescheduling over, it was this, right?

She'd opted for a plain gray skirt that cut off just above her knees and a black blouse with a tie around the neck, her hair tied up in a slick ponytail for the interview. Professional but stylish. Based on what she'd seen of Sandra Simone the night before, the woman appreciated style.

She and Miller were quiet as they climbed into his SUV and headed for the highway. Miller chewed on his sandwich as he drove, but despite missing lunch, Jo was far too nervous to have any kind of appetite. Then there was the whole issue of dinner later with her parents—but she couldn't even muster the energy to worry about that yet.

But stupidly, more than anything else, she couldn't stop thinking about the kiss. It had just been for show, obviously. Miller had seen her in distress with her parents and swooped in to rescue her, like the white knight he thought he was. It hadn't meant anything, and now that he was full-on pretending to be her boyfriend to get her parents to leave her alone, she was going to owe him big time.

But the last thing she'd expected was for the kiss to feel that...nice.

She stared out her window as he drove, forcing the memory away. She didn't want to think about how soft his lips had been, or the way his familiar scent had suddenly affected her differently than it ever had before. She didn't want to think about how strong his chest had felt under her hand, or how it had felt like the kiss was cut too short.

Eventually, Jo turned on the radio to drown out the silence, and pumped her leg up and down to the beat of the song.

What she should have been worrying about was this interview and what she was going to say. How she was going to win Sandra Simone over and convince her she was worthy of a job a thousand photographers would kill for.

But all she could think about was Miller's hand resting on the gear shift and how close it was to her leg.

"Thanks for saving me last night," she finally said.

The corner of his mouth turned up, but his eyes remained glued to the road. "You looked like you could use some backup. Honestly, I had thought you were kidding about your mom. But yeah, yikes."

"I think you just made her year. But don't feel like you have to come to dinner tonight. I can make up some excuse."

"Are you afraid I'm going to embarrass you?" he teased.

"Well, that's a given." Jo relaxed into her seat, the weird tension that had settled over the car finally easing. "What are you going to do if my interview runs long?"

"Jo. It's a huge bookstore. I'm good."

She snorted. "You're such a nerd."

"And you love it. Do you feel prepared for your interview? Want me to pop off some practice questions?"

"Oh, God, please don't. That'll just make me more nervous."

"What do you have to be nervous about? She asked you to come in after just a glance at your portfolio. She clearly likes you. In my book, you're already hired."

Jo sighed. "You didn't see her, Mill. She was all glamorous and shiny in person. The kind of person who looks impossible to impress."

"And yet...you've already impressed her."

"I think *impressed* is too strong of a word."

"Well, you look the part today. So if she's not impressed by the end of this, she clearly has no soul."

Jo rolled her eyes but smiled despite herself. "Can we talk about something else to distract me? What's going on in your life? How are your capstone projects going?"

Miller winced and flipped on the blinker to change lanes. "Let's just say I'll probably be pulling several all-nighters in the library this week. You wanna pay me back for this ride and come keep me company?" He grinned and batted his eyelashes at her as they took the exit.

"Me? In a library? I think we both know the answer to that."

Sandra's studio was in the quieter side of downtown. Luckily, Miller had no trouble finding a spot in the parking lot across the street. Unluckily, a light drizzle of rain had broken out, and judging by the thick, dark clouds looming above them, it was only going to get worse. Jo glanced at the clock—they were more than fifteen minutes early—but she didn't want to risk waiting out here and having to sprint through heavier rain later on, ruining her outfit and meticulously styled hair moments before interviewing with the most put-together woman she'd ever seen.

"Hold on." Miller restarted the car and eased out of the lot.

"What are you doing?" she demanded.

He glanced both ways down the empty street before pulling up to the curb in front of the studio with the chic black and white *Sandra Simone Photography* sign in the window.

"Go on then," he urged.

She gave his arm a quick *thank you* squeeze before hopping out of the car and hurrying under the overhang. She waved as Miller's car pulled off, and she braced herself with a deep breath before heading inside.

A woman Jo didn't recognize smiled at her from the front desk, large cat-eye glasses taking up the majority of her face. "Are you Johanna Palmer?" she asked.

Jo nodded. "I'm supposed to have an interview with Ms. Simone at two?" She wasn't sure why it came out like a question. She needed to get it together. If she wanted any shot of landing this, she had to go into that interview exuding confidence and competence.

"You can head on back. She's expecting you."

A cold blast of air conditioning swept over Jo as she pushed through the glass doors and paused outside Sandra Simone's office. The entire wall was transparent, exposing walls full of Sandra's photos, and a wide, white desk at the back. Sandra was typing something on her large desktop computer but paused and glanced up as Jo hesitantly ventured inside.

"Johanna!" Sandra stood and reached over the desk to offer her hand. Jo quickly crossed the rest of the space between them to shake it, forcing herself to make eye contact even though all she wanted to do was examine every inch of this office. One of Sandra's most famous shots stared back at her from the far wall—a close-up of a woman with thick, red juice dripping from every inch of her face.

Sandra looked different today than she had at the show-case, to a slightly jarring degree. She wore simple dark jeans and a black high-neck blouse, her wavy hair loose around her face. She smiled warmly and gestured for Jo to take one of the velvet green chairs across from her.

"So glad you could make it in on such short notice, but I knew the moment I saw your portfolio, if I didn't sweep you up fast, someone else would."

"I—thank you."

"We're looking for a summer intern, and I think you could be perfect for it. The position is paid—although to be fully transparent, it's still an intern salary. However, if you do well here, I'd be willing to revisit with you at the end of your internship about a full-time position, or at the very least, a recommendation letter. Are you planning to stay in town after graduation?"

"I haven't really made any concrete plans yet," said Jo. "Just trying to be flexible for whatever opportunities present themselves."

Sandra nodded approvingly and spun her monitor around so Jo could see. There was a bulleted list on one side and a calendar on the other with nearly every date filled with something or another.

"There are no wrong answers here," said Sandra, which immediately spiked Jo's nerves. "The position is already yours if you want it. But I want to gauge where you're at now and what you have experience with."

Jo relaxed a bit in her chair as Sandra spouted off question after question—talking about the logistics of photography was a lot less intimidating than trying to sell herself. She'd been glued to a camera since elementary school. Most of this was second nature by now. Sandra nodded and smiled along with each answer until finally turning the monitor around and leaning back in her chair.

"My assistant at the front will have some paperwork for you—feel free to take your time and look it over, and give me a call sometime next week if you think we might be a good fit."

"Absolutely." Jo rose to shake her hand again, her cheeks aching from the smile she couldn't seem to turn off.

Sandra walked her to the door but paused before Jo stepped into the hallway and let out a small laugh. "I just realized, you'll be in good company here. Sandra, Johanna, and my assistant out there is Brenda."

"We sound like an all-girl band."

"It's funny you should say that. Your name is beautiful, by the way, but I've never known a Johanna. I've only ever heard the name in a song my son wrote, actually."

Johanna's heart lurched to a stop. The smile froze on her face, and she swallowed hard before responding. "Your son—he's in a band?" Her voice rose steadily with each word.

"Oh, yes." Sandra beamed, oblivious to the cold sweat collecting on every inch of Jo's skin. "His name is Greyson. Don't even get me started on the name of their band, but their music seems to be popular with the younger crowds, and it pays the bills for him, so who am I to complain? I actually think his song 'Johanna' was his first big hit! Funny coincidences, huh?"

"Funny coincidences," Jo murmured, locking her hands together behind her back to hide their trembling.

"Have a good rest of your afternoon!" Sandra patted her on the back and poked her head out into the hallway. "Be careful though, it looks like it's pouring rain out there."

Jo nodded, a numbness sloggily filling her body as she stumbled out to the reception area and took the papers from Sandra's assistant. The woman smiled and said something Jo couldn't make out from the roaring in her ears, so

Jo just nodded and shoved the papers in her bag before heading outside.

The rain surged down, violently ricocheting off the sidewalk. The edges of Jo's vision blurred, and she realized she couldn't breathe. She sucked in shallow breath after breath, turning her head back and forth, suddenly so disoriented, she had no idea where to go.

It seemed no matter where she tried to go, there were just some things that would always follow her.

11

FRESHMAN YEAR - NOVEMBER

JOHANNA CLAMPED A HAND OVER HER MOUTH TO STIFLE a sob. She sank onto the cold bathroom tiles and pulled her knees to her chest, her eyes glued to the evidence in front of her.

Five of them.

She ripped another piece of toilet paper off to blow her nose and sucked in a calming breath. The moment her eyes landed on the pregnancy tests scattered around the floor, a new wave of hysterics threatened to drown her, so she shoved herself to her feet and pulled her phone from her pocket with shaking hands.

She and Grey had only exchanged a handful of texts since he left last month—barely a fraction of how much they used to talk. She'd taken the hint, but she couldn't *not* tell him.

Because there wasn't anyone else it could be.

The phone rang and rang, and she squeezed her eyes

THE ANTI-RELATIONSHIP YEAR   127

shut at the thought of leaving this on a voicemail. But if she chickened out now, she knew she'd never tell him. It needed to happen, and it needed to happen now.

"Johanna!" The phone crackled around his voice like he didn't have good reception. "It's good to hear from you! What's up?"

You might not think that in a minute.

"Do you have a second to talk?"

"For you, of course."

She pressed her forehead against the bathroom wall and squeezed her eyes shut until red stars burst behind her eyelids.

"Johanna? Are you there?" There was rustling on the other side of the phone, like he was walking around.

"Grey, I think I'm pregnant," she blurted.

For a moment, there was just silence. And then, very clearly: "What do you mean, *you think?*"

The flirty amusement was completely gone from his tone now.

She swallowed hard. "I mean I have five positive at-home tests in front of me."

Again, silence.

Her mind cartwheeled through a million possibilities of things to say.

I don't expect anything. I just thought you should know.

I'm sorry to have to tell you this over the phone.

I'm scared.

But more than anything, she just wanted him to say something.

"Look, Johanna." There was a coldness in the way he

said her name this time. "I really can't deal with this right now. We're about to get signed with this label." He sighed, and there was more rustling in the background. "Besides, it's probably not even mine anyway."

And then he hung up.

Jo stared at the phone in her hand, mouth open, eyes wide. Then her stomach dropped so violently she fell to her knees in front of the toilet, waiting for herself to be sick.

But all that came out were more tears.

Then she threw her head back and screamed.

She screamed and screamed and threw her phone against the wall, finding the smallest hint of satisfaction as it shattered and fell to the ground in broken pieces. She kicked the pregnancy tests on the floor, sending them flying against the walls. Then she crumbled to the floor once more, buried her face in her hands, and sobbed.

She froze at a knock on the door. No one else was supposed to be home right now. Kayleigh, Addie, and Liv all had class. She'd triple-checked before coming in here.

"Jo?" Miller. It was Miller's voice. He knocked again. "Can I come in? Are you all right?"

There was absolutely no explaining away her current state, so she just rested her forehead on her knees and mumbled, "It's unlocked."

The door creaked open, but she didn't look up. Footsteps drew closer, then she felt Miller sink onto the floor beside her. He must have seen the mess—the pregnancy tests, the dirty tissues, the broken phone—but he didn't say anything. She sniffled and finally forced herself to raise her head, but Miller wasn't staring at her like she'd expected. He had his knees tucked into his chest, his arms braced around them, and he was staring intently at the floor, his jaw flexing.

When he noticed she'd looked up, his features softened. "Do you want to talk about it?"

She wiped the back of her hand under her nose and stared at the pregnancy test closest to her feet. The plastic was now cracked down the middle, but its result was still perfectly clear. "I called Grey," she said tonelessly.

Miller glanced at her phone's remains on the ground. "What did he say?"

"That it's not his. Then he hung up."

Miller whipped around to look at her. "Are you fucking kidding me?"

She pressed her lips together and shook her head. "I just don't understand how this happened," she murmured, mostly to herself. "We used a condom."

Miller shifted uncomfortably. At first she thought it was just talking about sex, but then a muscle in his jaw jumped again, and he opened and closed his mouth like he was debating saying something.

"What?" she asked.

"Are you sure?"

"I—what do you mean?"

He hung his head and pinched the bridge of his nose with two fingers. "Jo—I—just—well, did you see him put on the condom? Or did you see it afterwards?"

Jo stared straight ahead, that awful drop in her stomach returning, and *fuck*, now the tears were coming back too.

"I'm sorry, I didn't mean to—" Miller touched her arm, and she collapsed into his side, the tears running freely down her face now. He wrapped his arm around her shoulders and pulled her tightly against him, his chin resting on the top of her head. "I'm sorry. I'm sorry. I'm sorry."

"Fuck." She covered her face with her hands. "I'm so *stupid*."

"No," he said firmly, his arm tightening around her. "You're not."

She swiped at the tears with the backs of her hands. His wide, blue eyes stared back at her. "I don't know what to do," she whispered.

He nodded, his brow furrowing. "Well, one thing at a time, right? We'll go to a doctor to know for sure, and we'll go from there."

She didn't know if he even realized his word choice, but just him saying *we* instead of *you* made the whole thing fractionally more bearable. She smiled, wiping the last of the tears from her face with shaking hands. "Right. Okay."

"I can't let you drive like this. I'll take you."

"You don't have to do that—"

"Well, I'm doing it, so."

She let out a shaky laugh and wiped her snot-covered hands on her jeans. "Miller?"

"Yeah?"

She leaned forward, threw her arms around his shoulders, and buried her face against his neck. His arms immediately wrapped around her back and pulled her against him, one hand stroking the back of her head. "It's going to be okay," he murmured. "It's going to be okay."

JO SAT SILENTLY IN THE CAR ON THE RIDE HOME FROM the doctor's office. Day slid into night as the appointment became a procedure, and the day forever changed from being just another Saturday to *The Saturday.* It was dark now, the entirety of the day gone, but Miller had sat there waiting the entire time, first in the waiting room as Jo stared at the floor and pumped out a nervous rhythm with her leg, and then in the office as the doctor explained her options, though the static in her ears had drowned out most of what she'd said.

He didn't say anything as they drove, and Jo stared out the window, wondering if she would feel anything, or if that wouldn't come until after she took the second medication. What if it didn't work at all, and she had to go through all of this again?

About halfway home, Miller flipped on the radio and hummed along. The low quality of his voice was calming, in a way. Jo closed her eyes, focusing on it, almost feeling the vibrations in her chest. It was about the only thing she *could* feel right now. The doctor had explained that all women reacted differently, emotionally. But for now, Jo just felt...numb. The kind of numbness that made her worry she'd never feel anything again.

They were just turning onto campus when the song on the radio ended.

"And now we have a new song from a local band!" said the host. "I think you guys are really going to like this one. Here's 'Johanna' by United Fates!"

Miller slammed on the breaks in the middle of the parking lot, and Jo had to brace her hands on the dashboard to keep from pitching forward. She let out a small choking noise as the song trickled through the speakers. She stared at the screen where *Johanna – United Fates* scrolled across over and over again. The numbness in her chest cracked, like a splinter fissuring through a block of ice.

Miller slammed his hand against the radio, cutting the song off midway through the first verse. A shake grew in Jo's chest, branching out from her chattering teeth to her trembling hands. But she didn't cry.

She didn't have any tears left.

"Let's go inside," Miller practically growled, but Jo was glued to the spot, eyes still trained on the radio. She couldn't face Addie or Liv or Kayleigh right now. She couldn't curl into a ball on her bed without questions and concerns that she didn't have the slightest amount of energy to deal with. Suddenly she wanted nothing more than to be back home where she could lock herself in her room and be completely and utterly alone. Maybe she'd sleep in her car tonight.

She shook her head slowly back and forth. "I can't—with them—"

"Come on," Miller said, his voice gentle this time, as he

got out of the car and opened her door. Shakily, she took his hand, and he wrapped an arm around her shoulders as he led her toward the building. "You can stay in my room. Alan went home for the weekend."

She didn't even bother arguing, and winced as they climbed the stairs, her hands wrapped firmly around her stomach as it started to cramp.

"Are you all right?" asked Miller.

She just gritted her teeth and nodded. Addie and Liv's laughter reverberated through the hall as they hurriedly slipped into Miller's room. It was the first time she'd seen it, she realized. He always came over to theirs. It looked like every other boy's dorm room, though Miller's side was noticeably more organized than his roommate's.

"Here." He rushed over to the bed and knocked off a pile of clothes. "You can sit up here. Don't worry, it's clean and everything. I just washed the sheets."

She immediately curled into a ball on her side, the cramping in her abdomen subsiding now that she wasn't moving around. It didn't hurt, exactly, or maybe she was just used to severe enough period cramps that it wasn't that far out of the ordinary. But there was a level of constant discomfort she hadn't experienced before.

"What do you need?" Miller was asking, his movements frantic as he hurried back and forth across the room, cleaning as he went. "What can I get you?"

"Do you have any ibuprofen?"

"Yes!" He grinned, looking relieved to have something that could help, and quickly brought her a bottle of pills and a glass of water.

"Do you have a heating pad?" she murmured.

The triumphant look on his face faltered.

"Never mind. You're a boy. Of course you don't."

"You know what? I'll run to the store. There's that one just around the corner. It'll take five minutes. What else do you need? Give me a list."

She pulled her knees closer to her chest. Maybe if she curled herself into a small enough ball, the cramps would leave her alone. "You don't have to do that."

Miller knelt down so his face was level with hers. "Give me a list, Jo."

She grimaced. "I'm gonna need more pads."

His expression didn't change. "What else?"

She reached for her pockets, then remembered she'd smashed her phone against the wall earlier. "That's it, but could I borrow your phone?"

He laid it on the bed, then strode to the dresser across from her, pulled out a pair of black sweats and a gray T-shirt, and laid them next to the phone. "Just, uh"—he shrugged—"if you want to change into something more comfortable. Okay. I'll be right back."

"Thanks, Miller," she whispered.

As he left, she pulled up his phone and dialed the phone number she'd had memorized by heart since she was thirteen. She pressed her face into the pillow as it rang.

"Hello?"

The familiar voice on the other line tipped her over the edge. The tears returned in full force, and she hiccuped a few times before finally managing to squeeze out, "Hi, Mare."

MILLER RETURNED TO THE ROOM WITH FOUR overstuffed plastic bags, eyes slightly frantic. He kicked the door shut behind him and immediately jumped into unpacking his purchases on the desk.

"So." He pulled out four different packages of pads and laid them out on the foot of his bed in a neat row. "I had no clue what *wings* were, so I got some with and some without. But then I realized there are different *sizes*, and you're tiny, so at first I thought, *yeah, of course she'd be the smallest one*, but then what if that was *wrong* and you wanted the bigger ones? So I got both. *Then* when I was looking for the heating pads—do you have any idea how many different ones there are?—so I got one that plugs in the wall, and this one you kind of just throw in the microwave." He set them beside the pads, then returned to digging through his bags. "So then I thought maybe you'd want some candy. But then I realized I don't know what kind you like! So I got all of them." With this, he dumped out the rest of the bags onto the bed, which did, indeed, have one of every single kind of candy in the store.

Jo stared at the mountain of sugar on the bed with wide eyes.

"So"—Miller's eyes flickered from the candy to Jo —"which ones do you like?"

She hesitantly reached forward and dug out the bag of Swedish Fish.

Miller's eyes practically bulged out of his head.

"Swedish *Fish?*" he demanded. "Of all of these, you chose *Swedish Fish?*"

She shrugged and ripped open the bag. He shook his head as if insulted, then pulled the heating pads out from under the mess. "I can plug this one in over here." He ducked under the bed to find an outlet and handed her the pad, then grabbed the second one to throw in the microwave. When he was done and finally paused to take a breath, he turned to face her with his hands on his hips. "Is this okay, then?"

A small smile crept onto her face. "You're a good friend, Mill. Oh!" She dug around in the blankets until she found his phone and handed it back to him. "Thank you."

"You get your call made?" he asked.

"Yeah. Just wanted to talk to a friend from home."

After clearing off the rest of the candy, he dug around in the plastic bins underneath his bed and came up with a handful of blankets and an extra pillow to make a spot on the floor.

"You don't want to use his?" She nodded at his roommate's bed.

Miller glanced up at her from the ground. "Trust me. It's more sanitary down here."

She rolled onto her side and adjusted the heating pad against her stomach. "You're sure this is okay?"

"Jo, it's fine. Just wake me up if you need anything else, okay?"

She rolled onto her back, trying to quiet her mind. The entire day was a blur, and she already couldn't remember parts of it. Just bits and pieces. It almost didn't feel real.

But the more she thought about it, the more the worst of the thoughts crept in, and she clenched her jaw, trying to force them to the back of her mind. Trying not to focus on anything but the uneven surface of the ceiling and Miller's deep, even breaths as he fell asleep.

12

SENIOR YEAR · MARCH

MILLER APPEARED AROUND THE CORNER WITH A PLASTIC bag with *Powell's Books* printed across the front. When he noticed Jo standing beside his locked car completely soaked, he broke into a run.

"What the hell, Jo?" he called, his voice barely audible above the rain. "Why didn't you come get me? Or text me?"

She shook her head, still unable to form words, and numbly climbed into the car. Water pounded against the windshield, blurring the parking lot in front of them. The entire sky was painted an angry shade of blue, and it didn't look like the storm was planning to let up anytime soon. She could still feel the steady drum of water on her skin, the coldness seeping all the way to her bones. It felt like she was underwater. Just floating. Floating and numb and cold.

Miller slid into the driver seat and looked her over as

he started the car and blasted the heat. Seeming to sense she wasn't in the mood for conversation, he eased the car out of the lot, the wipers flashing across the windshield as fast as they could go. Once he merged onto the highway, he finally glanced at her and asked, "What happened?"

Jo shrugged and turned, watching the water kicking up beneath the tires of the other cars. Sandra flashed behind her eyes. Her easy smile. The warmth of her handshake. The light in her eyes as she talked about her son. "She offered me a summer internship."

"What! Jo, that's amazing! I don't understand. Why don't you look more amazed right now?" When Jo didn't respond, he added, "Was she a total bitch or something?"

"No, she was really nice, actually."

"Then what's the problem?"

Jo faced forward again. A morphed version of her stared back at her from the windshield, her eyes not quite right. "Simone isn't her real last name," she murmured.

Miller paused, waiting for her to elaborate. "Uh —okay?"

Jo tilted her head, watching as her reflection mirrored the movement. Rain cut across her face, blurring all of her features, and she reached up to touch her own lips. They were still cold to the touch. "Her last name is Carter."

"I'm not following."

Jo closed her eyes. "Carter as in Greyson Carter."

"You mean...? You're fucking kidding me."

A small, hard laugh escaped Jo's throat. "I'm about to lose my mind. I'm losing my fucking mind. Like what the actual *fuck*?" Her voice broke at the end, and then she was laughing. She was laughing so hard she couldn't breathe. She leaned forward, clutching her stomach with both hands, gasping for air.

"Jo. Jo, you're scaring me."

She sucked in a deep breath and leaned back in the chair, letting her eyes close as the back of her head hit the leather. "I'm fine," she said. "It just...threw me off, I guess."

"Understandably. You're really okay?"

She nodded and opened her eyes again, the word *okay* bouncing around in her head. It felt like the right word. She *was* okay. Happy? No. But okay? She'd just been given the one opportunity she wanted most. Grey had already taken too many things away from her. She wasn't going to let him take this way too, no matter his relation to Sandra.

"You want to stop and get fries on the way back?" Miller offered.

Jo smiled. There were few problems in this life potatoes couldn't solve. As she opened her mouth to respond, the car swerved, and the driver on their right blared their horn. Jo jerked to the side, and her shoulder slammed into the door. Miller frantically turned the wheel as the car fishtailed back and forth. Car horns surrounded them as water splashed up from the road, coating the windshield.

Miller cursed under his breath and yanked the car onto the shoulder of the highway, jostling them violently as the car transitioned onto the dirt. Something *thudded* against the bottom of the car as Miller turned the hazard lights on and eased the car as far away from the road as he could manage.

"What's wrong?" Jo gasped, her heart still stuck somewhere in her throat.

"I think it's a flat."

Of course. *Of course* that would happen today. Miller shut off the car, making the wipers freeze halfway across the windshield, and pressed his forehead against the steering wheel.

"You don't have a spare, do you?" Jo asked quietly.

He gave the smallest shake of his head as the noise from the rain pounding on the car's roof filled the space between them. Cars roared past them on the road, fast enough to shake the car. Jo sucked in a shallow breath, but it did nothing to calm her nerves. She needed *air.* Jo threw her door open, and the rain immediately assaulted her.

"Jo, what are you doing?" Miller called. "Get back in the car! It's not safe!"

But she'd already slammed the door shut and circled to the back, the rain immediately soaking through her clothes and plastering her hair to her neck. She glanced down the small hill that ended in a patch of trees below them. The ground was slick beneath her feet, the dirt already turning to mud.

Suddenly, it was all too much. This day, this place, this —everything. She just needed some air. She just needed to *breathe*, but nothing she inhaled seemed to quite reach her lungs.

She heard a car door open behind her and realized she'd ventured farther down the shoulder, her shoes brushing the edge of the drop-off, the incline steeper than she'd first realized.

Miller called out to her, but his words were lost to the rain and speeding cars. Jo ducked away as one hit a nearby puddle and sent the water flying toward her.

"I just need a minute!" she yelled, her voice immediately swept away by the storm. She wrapped her arms around herself and tilted her head back to feel the rain on her face.

"It's not safe out here." Red reflected off Miller's face with each flash of the hazard lights as he walked toward her. "I called for a tow."

He reached for her, but she took another step back and shook her head.

"I just need a minute," she insisted.

Something like frustration flashed across his face. "Jo, get in the car."

He reached for her again, and this time when she went to step away, she felt the mud slip out from under her foot. Her ankle twisted to the side, pitching her body backwards. Her arms flailed around her, and she felt Miller's hand slide against hers, but still, she fell.

Her hip connected with the ground first, sending shockwaves of pain through her bones. She rolled, her body picking up speed as she went, and reached out desperately for something to stop herself as mud and water flew up around her. She landed on her back at the bottom of the hill, the breath momentarily knocked clear from her lungs.

"*Jo!*"

She blinked up, vision blurry from the fall or the rain,

she wasn't sure. A tall figure slid down the muddy embank-ment and landed on his knees beside her.

A dull ache radiated through her body, numbed by the cold. Miller's hands found each side of her head. Rain dripped from his face as he leaned forward. "Are you hurt?"

She turned her head to the side to spit the mud out of her mouth. "Shit," she groaned.

"Can you stand?"

Holding on to his arms, Jo pulled herself into a seated position, then pulled her legs up to stand. The moment she put pressure on her ankle, a new wave of pain tore through her, and she collapsed. Miller caught her before she could fall and murmured something unintelligible before sweeping her into his arms. She hissed in pain and hooked her arms around his neck, pressing her face against his cold, wet skin as he paused and looked up the muddy slope. Headlights continued to flash by as Miller's hazard lights blinked *on, off, on, off, on, off.*

He started up the hill, sliding back in the mud with each step, the rain angled directly into their faces.

With a grunt, he lunged up the last few feet and crested the hill, landing beside the car on his knees. By the time he managed to wrestle Jo into the SUV's back seat, they were both soaked, covered in mud, and slightly out of breath. He climbed in after her and shut the door, enclosing them into a muffled sort of quiet. Jo's ears rang.

Miller pulled out an old sweatshirt to wipe the mud from his face as best he could, then handed it to her. "Let me see it." He pulled her leg onto his lap as she dabbed the sleeve against her neck. He glanced toward the trunk. "I think I have a first aid kit in here somewhere."

"I think it's just twisted," she said, but gritted her teeth as he moved her foot to inspect the damage.

His hands paused on her calf as he looked up at her, and she braced herself. But instead of the *what the hell were you thinking*, or *I told you so*, she was expecting, he said, "Are you all right? Does anything else hurt?"

Headlights flashed across the car, momentarily illuminating his profile. She shook her head. "I'm fine, Mill," she said quietly.

A corner of his lips curved. "Is now a bad time to tell you that you look like hell?"

She kicked him lightly in the chest with her good foot. "You don't look much better."

He grabbed her good ankle before she could pull her leg back and pulled her toward him. "Don't think just because you're injured, I won't retaliate." She landed beside him on the center seat, both legs on his lap. He reached forward and took a piece of her blouse with two fingers. The tie had come loose, and there was now a long rip in the neckline. "Sorry about your fancy outfit."

She met his gaze, the blue of his eyes stark in contrast to the smear of mud from his temple to the opposite cheekbone. His lips parted, and she felt herself drawing closer without making the conscious choice to. And then there was no distance left between them at all, and he exhaled against her lips as she brought her mouth to his.

He froze, his entire body going rigid beneath her, and she immediately pulled back. She stared at him, wide-eyed.

THE ANTI-RELATIONSHIP YEAR

"I'm sorry—I don't know why I—"

He grabbed her face with both hands and crushed his lips to hers. At first, it was overwhelming. All-consuming. The heat of his skin and his breath. The hurried desperation as they crashed together. She immediately opened her mouth to him, his scent wrapping around her as his hands slid up her back, and she leaned into his chest. She'd been kissed a million times before, but not like this. His mouth devoured hers as if he were starving for her. She fisted her hands in his hair, pulling herself as close to his body as she could manage as his tongue swept into her mouth.

The car jostled around them as other drivers roared past, and the rain hammered on the roof overhead. But the more she breathed Miller in, the more she tasted him and felt his hands explore her skin, the more everything around them dimmed to a low hum.

His teeth sank into her lower lip with enough intensity to make her gasp, then his lips trailed to her jaw, her neck, his fingers pulling at the tie in her hair until it came free. She drew herself up, pulling one leg over to straddle his lap. She paused, her lips barely an inch from his, and he blinked up at her with hooded eyes, his chest rising and falling with each breath.

She'd never known him like this, *seen* him like this. And a part of her felt like maybe she was intruding somewhere she didn't belong.

He spoke a single word, the sound barely audible over the rain. A breathy, desperate thing, as he felt her about to pull away.

"Don't."

She ran the tips of her fingers along his face—his eyebrows, his cheekbones, his lips, laughing softly as she brushed away the leftover mud—a face that had grown nearly as familiar to her as her own these past few years. And the way he was looking at her, the openness in his eyes, she couldn't breathe. She couldn't think, except to wonder if he'd looked at her like this all along, and she'd just never noticed.

"Miller," she whispered.

His eyes fell closed. "Don't."

His mouth collided with hers again, and she let herself fall into it. One of his hands cupped the back of her neck, and the other slid around her ribs. Then she was on her back, his weight pressing into her as his mouth glided across her jaw, her neck, her shoulder, her lips.

She tugged on the back of his shirt, and he pulled back just enough for her to yank it over his head. She gasped as their movements turned into a frantic dance, his hands desperately searching for every inch of her skin as she pulled her blouse over her head. He buried his face in the crook of her neck for a moment as his hand drifted down her arm until he reached her wrist, then slid his fingers through hers. Everywhere he touched, he left her skin on fire and desperate for more.

"Jo," he whispered.

The fire spread, pulsing, *aching*, until she arched against him like she'd already grown addicted to the feel of his body on hers. She could feel his heart pounding against his chest, his breaths coming in short gasps against her skin.

She reached for the clasp on his jeans, and he kissed her harder, deeper.

A knock on the window echoed through the car.

Jo's breath caught in her throat as Miller lurched off her and steadied himself against the front seats. Jo's arms flew up to cover herself as she shielded her eyes from the flashlight pointed directly at them. Miller leaned to the side, blocking Jo from view as a man in a red hat squinted in.

"Did one of you call for a tow?"

13

FRESHMAN YEAR - DECEMBER

Jo vaguely wondered if the sink would break out from under her. Frat bathrooms were never in the best shape, but this one was even rougher than usual. One of the stalls had a door hanging from a single hinge, the walls clearly had water damage, and *thank God* it was too dark to see the floor clearly. Unfortunately, the guy fingering her clearly had no idea what the fuck he was doing, so she had little else to do than look around.

"All right," she finally said, pushed him away by the chest, and readjusted her clothes. The door opened as another couple stumbled inside, and pulsing music from the party poured into the room.

"What?" The guy stumbled back—Jo had no idea what his name was. He was so drunk that when he reached for the wall, he missed by at least two feet, and stumbled back against the bathroom stalls.

"I'm going to get another shot!" Jo called and jabbed her thumb toward the door.

The guy nodded like he wanted to come with her, but she slipped out of the bathroom and plunged into the crowd of sweaty, drunken college students before he could catch up.

She'd lost the girls she'd come here with tonight—Lacy and Tracy, the twins who ran the photograph club—but she hadn't found their company particularly enjoyable anyway. The pledge behind the bar grinned at her as she approached. The brothers had him wearing a bikini top and a sombrero, even though Jo was pretty sure the theme for tonight was James Bond.

"Another shot?" he asked.

"Tequila!" Jo yelled over the music as she gathered her hair behind her neck and yanked it into a ponytail. A sheen of sweat had broken out across her skin.

The pledge poured two shots—one for her, and one for himself, apparently. He was cute, she supposed, but the bikini top was hard to look past. He raised the shot glass, clanked it against hers, and she threw it back, not even tasting it. She locked eyes with a guy down the bar, who nodded at her. She quickly turned away and scanned the crowd. No sign of Lacy or Tracy. Maybe they left. And now that the E she'd taken earlier was wearing off, this party was suddenly a lot less fun.

Hands grabbed her hips and pulled her back against a body. "You wanna dance?" an unfamiliar voice murmured in her ear.

"Nope." She shook off the stranger's hands and pushed

back into the crowd, the room a little blurrier than it had been before. Two girls who looked a lot like Addie and Liv were dancing on some guys in the corner, and Jo quickly pivoted away, not wanting to deal with them tonight either. The song shifted as she reached the center of the dance floor, and she froze, the alcohol that had been burning in her chest a moment ago instantly turning to ice.

She wants to get a taste, oh yeah she wants it, we all know.

She's got that pretty face, I shouldn't go there, no, no, no—

The room blurred around her, darkening around the edges. She shoved her way through the crowd toward the exit, her heartbeat hammering in her ears.

Red hair, leather jacket.

Maybe I should let her have it.

She sucked in a lungful of air as she plunged out the side door. The night was cold, but every inch of her skin felt like it was on fire. She scowled at the line of people waiting on the driveway—it would take forever to get a DD. The music pulsed out onto the lawn, and she covered her ears, trying to block out the words.

When that didn't work, she started walking.

"Where are you going?" someone yelled after her, but she ignored them and headed across the backyard while simultaneously trying to get her phone out of her bra. She squinted at the screen, trying to force her vision to focus, and jabbed the call button, hoping she'd found the right contact.

"Hello?" Miller's voice was rough, like she'd just woken him up. She squinted again at the screen, trying to see the time.

"I'm sorry, I shouldn't—have called. It's late."

"Jo?" There was rustling in the background. "Where are you?"

"I'm f-fine. I'm just gonna *walk* home."

"Walk home?" Miller's voice was clearer now, louder. "Jo, it's like ten degrees outside. Where are you?"

"It's only like a block from the frat houses. I'll be *finnnne.*"

"Jo, that's like three miles. I'm coming to get you."

Jo paused on the sidewalk and glanced both ways. The street was utterly empty, and her vision was too blurry to see the signs. "Which way do I go again?"

"*Jo,*" Miller snapped, his voice suddenly hard. "*Stop* walking. Go inside somewhere. I'm leaving the dorm now."

"It's a little cold out here," she mumbled.

"You think?"

"Miller." She sighed, paced back over to the grass, and laid down. The entire world wobbled around her, the ground bobbing up and down like she was on a boat. "I'm a *liiiiittle* drunk."

"I can tell."

She pushed her bottom lip out. "Are you mad?"

"No, Jo, I'm not mad." She heard a car engine roar to life on the other end of the phone. "Are you inside?"

"I'm in some grass."

"For fuck's sake," he muttered. "Okay, I'm using Find My Friends. I'll be there in five minutes."

"Can people freeze to death in five minutes?"

"Not people who *go inside.* What are you wearing out there anyway?"

"*Ooooh*, what are *you* wearing?"

"Jo."

She sighed, put the phone on speaker, and tossed it aside so she could run her hands through the grass. It was hard and crunchy, like it had frosted over, and she realized her teeth were chattering. Maybe a tube top hadn't been the right call. But it had been so *hot* inside the party.

"You have a hot over-the-phone voice, Miller," Jo murmured. "You should be a phone sex operator."

He made a choking sound.

She wasn't sure how much time passed before headlights appeared on her right, and Jo sat up, squinting against them. If it wasn't Miller, whoever was behind the wheel was probably going to think she was dead lying there. She climbed to her feet, then doubled back for her phone. When she turned around again, the car was stopped in the middle of the street, and the driver's side door flew open. Miller appeared in pajama pants, bare feet, and a hoodie. He hurried toward the sidewalk, yanking his hoodie off as he went, even though he wasn't wearing anything underneath. Before Jo could react, he tugged the sweatshirt over her head.

She blinked at him—or the two versions of him—standing in front of her. He had *abs*? Since when did Miller have *abs*?

"Come on." He led her toward the passenger side, and she immediately moaned as she slid into the seat. The heat was cranked all the way up, and he already had her seat warmer on. She curled into a ball and snuggled into his sweatshirt as he climbed back into the car. Did all boys' sweatshirts smell this good, or was it just Miller's?

He didn't say anything as he drove them back to campus, and she studied his profile, searching for hints of anger.

"I'm sorry," she murmured.

"It's fine, Jo. I'm just glad you're okay."

He looked like he meant it too. Despite it being the middle of the night, despite this not being the first time she'd called him for something like this, despite him now being half naked in below-freezing temperatures because of her.

As he pulled into the parking lot and shifted the car into park, Jo's body reacted before she could think twice. She climbed onto his lap.

His eyes widened. "Jo—"

She grabbed his face with both hands and pressed her mouth to his, and for a moment, he didn't move. His entire body was stiff, his hands frozen in the air. But after one second passed, then two, his hands slowly fell to her waist, and his mouth opened. His breath came out shakily. Jo ran her fingers through his hair and pressed herself against his chest as she swept her tongue across his. And for a moment, she felt like she could melt into him. He was safe and warm and *good* and—

His hands tightened around her waist, and he pulled back.

She blinked up at him. "What's wrong?"

His jaw tightened, and a line formed between his eyebrows. "You're drunk," he said.

"Well, obviously." She didn't see what that had to do with anything.

He swallowed hard and looked away. "Let's get you inside."

As he opened the door and climbed out from under her, she sank back into the driver seat, her chest suddenly much heavier than it was before. Her eyes stung, and for a moment, she couldn't move. She couldn't *breathe*.

Miller knelt in front of her, forcing his face into her line of sight. He looked into her eyes, his jaw set off to the side, and for moment, just the smallest flicker of a second, his eyes dropped to her lips. But then his expression hardened, his eyes closing off to her. "Jo. I don't want to do this when you're drunk. If you woke up tomorrow and regretted it, I would never forgive myself, okay?" He brushed her hair away from her face. "Now will you please let me take you inside? It's freezing."

She nodded and stumbled out of the car, tripping over the stupid wedges she'd worn tonight. She stumbled and pitched forward, but Miller's arms shot out and wrapped around her waist, steadying her against his chest.

"Shit, Jo," he murmured. Then without warning, he swept her into his arms and started carrying her toward the dorm.

Jo had to squeeze her eyes shut for a moment, waiting for the world to stop spinning. She buried her face against Miller's chest and muttered, "I hate that fucking song."

When they reached her room, he set her back on her feet so he could wrestle the door open. She stumbled inside, running directly into her desk by the door, and let out a string of curses as she lurched forward. Miller caught her around the waist before she had a chance to hit the ground, and in doing so, *he* ran into the desk, this time knocking it back hard enough that it slammed into Jo's bedframe with an audible *thunk*.

"Ow," Jo complained as she hit the ground on her knees, Miller practically on top of her.

"Goddamn it!" The desk lamp on Kayleigh's side of the room flickered on, and she glared down at them from her bed. At least, Jo thought she was glaring. Her vision was still a little too blurry to be certain. "Are you *kidding* me right now?"

"Sorry, sorry," said Miller as he slid his arms under Jo and lifted her upright. "This will just take a minute."

"Sorry, Kayleigh," Jo slurred, swaying on her feet.

"You should've just left her there," Kayleigh muttered, then snapped off the light, casting the room back into darkness.

"She's mad," Jo whispered.

"Come on." Miller steadied her against the bed and sifted through her desk until he found the switch for her lamp. Jo squinted at the light, fingers futilely trying to undo the button on her jeans.

She threw her head back against the bed and groaned. "I can't sleep in these."

"Jo," Kayleigh growled, her voice half muffled by the pillow. "I swear to God—"

"Here." Miller lifted her onto the mattress, his entire head pointedly turned the other way as he finished unbuttoning her jeans for her and pulled them off her legs.

"Are you mad at me, too?" Jo whispered.

"No, Jo," Miller murmured as he helped her slide between the sheets. "I'm not mad."

He turned to leave, and she reached out to grab his wrist. He paused, his other hand hovering over her lamp as he met her eyes. She couldn't think of anything to say, so she just looked at him. He squeezed her hand gently and flipped off the light. "Good night, Jo."

"Good night, Miller," she whispered as the door clicked shut behind him.

Jo woke up the next morning to a small army trying to break out the front of her skull. She rolled over with a groan and desperately reached around her bedside table for some water. Her stomach roiled, and she clamped a hand over her mouth until the feeling passed. She glanced down to find herself in a sweatshirt she didn't recognize and no pants. She was still wearing underwear, so that was a good sign. As she twisted to inspect her face in the mirror, she caught a whiff of the sweatshirt.

Miller.

It had to be Miller's.

But when had she seen Miller last night?

If she ended the night in his sweatshirt, he must have come to her rescue again. He must have been *so* angry with her. Pushing her hair back from her face, she froze, hands flying to her ears. Her notably *naked* ears.

As if summoned by her thoughts, there was a light knock on her door, and Miller poked his head in.

"Oh, good. You're up." He stepped all the way into the room, and Jo realized Kayleigh wasn't here. Her entire side of the room looked untouched—bed made, desk clean, bag gone. Maybe she was with that guy she started seeing a few weeks ago.

"How are you feeling?" Miller asked.

Jo pointed to her ears. "Did you take off my earrings last night?"

His forehead wrinkled. "Was I...supposed to?"

Jo slumped back against the wall. "I guess I lost them. Damn, those were my favorite hoops. What happened last night? Please tell me I didn't do anything too embarrassing."

Miller shifted by the door, but didn't say anything at first. "You...don't remember any of it?"

She reached for her water bottle again. "Not much past the fifth tequila shot. I didn't throw up on you, did I?"

He looked away and scratched the back of his neck.

"Oh my God!" Jo covered her mouth with her hands. "Did I *throw up on you?*"

"No, no." Miller shook his head, finally raising his eyes to meet hers. "Nothing like that. I did have to come find you laying in the middle of a field last night, though."

Jo scrunched her nose. Maybe that's why her skin felt so itchy. "What the fuck was I doing in a field?"

"Hell if I know. But it was like ten degrees last night and you were insisting that you wanted to walk home."

Jo motioned to the sweatshirt. "I'm assuming that's where this comes in."

He nodded then looked away again. Hopefully she didn't flash him or something last night. But her jeans appeared to be in a pile on the floor next to her bed, so at least she'd waited until she got home to start undressing.

"Do you hate me?" she asked.

He stared at her for a second, and there was something behind his eyes she couldn't understand. It was like he was...*deciding* something. But then his expression relaxed back to his usual smirk, and he rolled his eyes. "Of course not. Now would you get dressed so we can go get breakfast? I'm starving."

❧ 14 ❧

SENIOR YEAR - MARCH

Jo's parents picked her up in their rental car shortly after the tow driver dropped her off at her apartment, leaving her little time to get ready for dinner. Besides jumping in the shower to rinse off the mud, throwing on a nice dress, pulling her wet hair into a bun, and wiping off the smeared makeup under her eyes, she hadn't been able to do much. Especially now that she was limping slightly from her ankle. Her mother tsked as she climbed in the car, but didn't comment.

Jo sat quietly in the backseat until they reached the restaurant. Her mind had gone from a dizzying kaleidoscope of thoughts to...nothing, like her system had finally gotten too overwhelmed and shut down. She numbly followed along as a host in a crisp black uniform showed them toward a round table at the back, right next to the windows. It looked out at the restaurant's terrace, which was strung up with twinkle lights. A fire pit sat at the center, surrounded by intricately carved benches for seating.

Her parents chatted about their flight next week to Denmark as they ordered a bottle of wine and picked up their menus. Jo stared at the empty seat across from her with unfocused eyes, the room in front of her barely registering.

She was still back in the car. Rain hammering down all around them. Miller's skin hot against her own. His breath on her neck. His voice in her ear. His lips—

"Where's Miller?"

Her father's voice snapped her back to the present, and she blinked at him.

"He—uh—might not be able to make it after all. Something came up."

Her mother's face fell. She licked her lips before leaning forward and dropping her voice to a whisper. "Did he break up with you?"

"God, Mom." Jo rolled her eyes and leaned back in her chair as the waiter reappeared with three glasses and a bottle of red wine. She wasn't particularly fond of the stuff, but figured her parents would disapprove if she started throwing back shots of tequila just to make it through the evening with them. Judging by the wine's label, it wasn't cheap.

Her mother shrugged innocently before picking up her glass and swishing the liquid around. Her father was typing something furiously on his phone. She waited halfheartedly for either of them to ask how her interview had gone—not that she wanted to talk about it, but it was the principle of the matter—but then the waiter reappeared to take their orders.

Her father finally glanced up from his phone, looking startled for a minute, like he'd forgotten where he was. He glanced from Jo to the empty seat beside her. "Where's Miller?" he asked.

"You already asked that," Jo reminded him, stifling a yawn.

"Oh." He frowned.

"Sorry I'm late."

Jo felt him before she saw his face. His hand skimmed her back as he slid into the seat beside her, a wave of shampoo hitting her as he passed. She stared at a suit-clad Miller with wide eyes as he reached over to shake her father's hand.

"My car got a flat, and it took forever at the shop." He pushed back his hair as he took his seat, Jo's mother cooing at him all the while about how she hoped everything was okay, and how they understood, and it was *so* good to see him, despite having just met him the day before.

Miller smiled along politely, and it wasn't until the waiter reappeared with another wine glass that Miller finally looked up and met Jo's gaze. For a moment, they just stared at each other. Jo wondered if his mind was as much of a tangled mess as hers was. If the same images were flashing behind his eyes. If he could still feel her on his skin the way she could feel him.

If the turmoil and confusion inside of him was so violent he also felt like he was on the verge of being sick.

He smiled, the gesture slow and soft, just the barest

curl of the corners of his mouth. She felt herself smiling back before she realized it, and the tight ball of heat in the center of her chest somehow eased and magnified at the same time.

"So, Miller," said Jo's mom. "Are you from Oregon?"

He held the eye contact for another beat before glancing over at her mom. "California. But I moved up here to actually experience more than one season for once."

Jo's mom laughed much more than the joke warranted, practically glowing under Miller's attention. "Are your parents excited for graduation?"

"Yeah, my mom and sister are coming. Don't worry, you won't be able to miss them. They'll be the ones screaming and possibly getting kicked out."

"And your father?" her mom pressed.

Jo widened her eyes, trying to get her mom's attention, but she was leaned forward, head propped in one hand, fully fixated on Miller.

Miller's smile stayed intact, though some tension crept into the creases around his eyes. "No, uh, he won't be there."

"Oh, that's too bad." Jo's mom reached over and squeezed her husband's arm. "We would've loved to meet him. Is he working?"

Jo tried to kick her under the table, but their seats were too far apart.

"My dad's not in the picture, actually." Before Jo's mom had the chance to push, as they both knew she would, he added, "He's in prison, and my mom has a restraining order against him."

The color immediately drained from her mom's face, and she opened and closed her mouth. "I—I'm so sorry."

"It's okay," Miller assured her. "He hasn't been around since my sister Alice was born, and my mom's amazing, so we were definitely better off."

Jo's mom swallowed nearly half of her glass of wine in a single gulp.

"What does your mother do?" Jo's dad offered.

"She's a therapist. She specializes in domestic abuse victims."

A heavy blanket of silence settled over the table, and Jo's eyes darted from Miller to her mom, desperately searching for a way to change the subject.

"She sounds amazing," Jo's mom finally said. "I hope we have the chance to meet her at graduation."

Apparently unperturbed by her previous misstep, Jo's mom wasted no time before jumping back in and lobbing more questions at Miller, but he handled them all with ease, the smile never leaving his face. He reached over and brushed his fingers against Jo's knee, then left them there, just the smallest hint of contact, but it burned right through her skin.

As the meal wrapped up, Miller offered to give her a ride back with him, and she agreed, though the idea of getting back in that car made her stomach tighten. They lingered on the terrace behind the restaurant and waved as Jo's parents pulled away. The night was cool, and it was too cloudy to make out any stars. Even the moon was barely visible. They stood in silence for a while, the only sound coming from the bubbling fountain behind them.

"Here." He was sliding the jacket of his suit over her shoulders before she even realized she'd been shivering, and she huddled into the collar.

"Thanks," she said quietly.

"It looks better on you anyway." He rolled his shirt-sleeves up to the elbows and wrapped his hands around the metal gate in front of them, the cords of muscles in his forearms straining as he tightened his grip. He stared ahead at the faintest outline of the city. Jo turned around and leaned her back against the railing, crossing her arms over her chest.

"That could've gone worse, right?" he finally said.

She laughed. "Yeah, I guess it could have. Sorry about my mom, though."

He laughed. "She's...passionate."

Another beat of silence passed between them, and she dropped her gaze to her feet. "I wasn't sure if you'd show up tonight."

"Of course I did," he said immediately. "I told you I would."

She swallowed, lost for a response. The air was slowly growing thicker between them, the silence heavier with each passing moment. "Your car's okay then?"

He nodded and twisted around, propping his body next to hers, close enough that their shoulders touched. She was hyperaware of the contact in a way she'd never been before, until the press of his body against hers was all she could feel. "Ready to head home?"

She nodded and pulled his jacket tighter around her shoulders as she leaned away from him, breaking the contact. Her hair was still slightly damp, and with every gust of the breeze that swept across the terrace, a new chill buried itself beneath her skin.

She couldn't meet Miller's eyes as they climbed into the car, and she sat up straight, refusing to let her eyes drift to the back seat. Miller cleared his throat as he started the car and pulled out of the parking lot wordlessly, drumming his fingers against the steering wheel as he drove. The restaurant wasn't far from their apartment building, barely a few miles, but the drive seemed to stretch on forever, the silence building into something else with each passing moment.

Were they supposed to act like it never happened? Or maybe it would be better to talk about it and just get it out of the way. But even then, what would she say? The entire car smelled the way his skin had, and it was impossible to think while her head was full of it.

It was impossible to think about any of this at all. Every time she tried, her entire body repelled the idea, blocking and repressing the memories with a desperate ferocity.

She jumped out of the car the moment he pulled into the parking lot and hurried toward the building.

"Jo!" A car door slammed behind her, followed by heavy footsteps, but this only made her quicken her pace. Suddenly she was frantic to get inside, frantic to get away from this feeling that was consuming every inch of her. "Jo!" Miller called again, his footsteps right behind her now.

She pushed through the front door and headed for the stairwell, her body too full of anxious energy to stand still in an elevator right now. Miller followed after her, but instead of stopping at the first floor to head to his apartment, he followed her up flight after flight until they reached the sixth floor.

He didn't call out to her again, now following behind silently until they reached her apartment in the middle of the hall. Her hands fumbled with the keys, trying to get it in the lock. Miller calmly reached over, laying his hand over hers, and twisted the knob.

She froze, the apartment door now cracked open, and stared at its wooden surface. Miller sighed and leaned against the wall next to her, his eyes on his hands. "Can I come in?" he asked quietly.

She nodded, still unable to speak, and stepped inside. Miller slipped in after her, closing the door behind them.

"Jo."

A beat of silence passed. She met his eyes, and then he had her pressed against the wall, his lips melding with hers. She gasped, frozen for only a second before she relaxed against him and twisted her fingers into his hair. *God*, it was even more all-consuming than the last time. His hips grinded against hers, his tongue filling her mouth, his hands gliding up and down her body like he was desperate to touch every part of her and couldn't get there fast enough.

The smallest trace of moonlight trickled in through the windows on the far wall, offering the only light in the room. Jo kicked off her shoes, adding another four inches to their height difference, and Miller immediately reached down, cupping the backs of her thighs with his hands, and hoisted her into his arms, her back still firmly pressed against the wall. Her dress hiked up around her hips as she locked her legs around him, knotted her hands in his hair, and pulled his head back so their lips were an inch apart.

"Bedroom," she whispered.

He nodded, crushing his lips back to hers as he carried her down the hall. She unbuttoned the collar of his shirt as he ducked into her bedroom, yanking impatiently at the fabric. He set her on the edge of the bed and bent over her to pull his jacket from her shoulders, his mouth now trailing to her neck. She finished with the rest of his buttons, and he rose back to his full height as he tossed his shirt aside.

And for a moment, it was all Jo could do to look at him. He'd filled out a bit since freshman year. Fundamentally, he looked about the same, but it was like she'd never seen him before. She rose up slowly in front of him, her hand skimming over the flat planes of his stomach, and he shivered under her touch. He watched her, his lips parted, as she reached up and pulled the tie from her hair. The damp, wavy strands collapsed around her shoulders, the floral smell of her shampoo filling the space between them. She turned to face the bed and glanced at him over her shoulder.

"Could you get my zipper?"

He gathered her hair in his hands and gently swept it over her shoulder, his hands lingering on her skin for a moment before trailing to the zipper at the center of her spine and slowly pulling it down until he reached her lower back. His breath brushed the back of her neck as he leaned forward and pressed his lips to her shoulder. His fingers slipped under the strap of her dress on the opposite side. Her eyes fluttered shut as he slid the strap down, then trailed his lips across her back until he reached her opposite shoulder, his fingers finding the remaining strap, and the dress pooled at her feet.

Miller sucked in a sharp inhale, his breath coming out shaky against the back of her neck. "Turn around," he whispered.

She complied, biting her lip as she lifted her head. His eyes didn't roam her body in the hungry way most men did. He stared right back, his gaze locked on hers, his chest rising and falling with each rapid breath. But when he brought his mouth back to hers, this kiss was slower, softer. A careful, deliberate exploration of her mouth, his hands slowly sliding up her back as her fingers unclasped his belt. He paused and pulled away an inch as she unfastened it, his eyes still closed.

"Are you sure?" he whispered.

It was a question she'd been asked several times before, but this time felt different. More loaded. This was Miller. *Her* Miller. And this was a line that couldn't be uncrossed.

But maybe it already had.

Maybe they'd been heading this way for a long time, and she'd chosen to turn a blind eye, because Miller was like a foundation. A safe place to land that she could always come back to. And shifting that, shifting *this* between them, maybe it would make the whole thing crumble.

But maybe there was a reason the first word that popped into her head when she thought about kissing him was *inevitable*, and the fear didn't come as readily as it once had. Maybe the only reason why it had any space in her head at all anymore was because she kept inviting it in.

She nodded and pulled him back to kiss him again, trailing her fingers down to the zipper on his pants. He sighed against her mouth, cupped the back of her head with his hands, and pushed them both back onto the bed.

As his weight pressed her into the mattress, her mind finally, mercifully, started to quiet. For now, this was all there was. All that was important. She could drown herself in this feeling, this skin against skin, the mouths and teeth and tongues and gasps—and everything else could wait.

The tightness in her chest she'd had since the interview, the anxious buzzing of thoughts that grew louder every day they drew closer to graduation, the nauseating pit in her stomach every time she had to meet the disinterested gazes of her parents, Miller melted it all away like fire. His hands slid from her waist to her hips and the tension in her chest eased a notch. His teeth grazed along the hollow of her throat, and it eased a little more. His fingers slid between her legs, and she closed her eyes, letting the rest of it slip away.

She reached for his pants, but he took her wrists and pinned them to the bed.

"Not yet," he breathed. "Just—let me."

The smallest flash of uncertainty and self-consciousness tightened in her chest. Men had gone down on her plenty of times before—dozens of men, if she were being honest.

But the thought of it being Miller—*Miller*, Miller—made her cheeks warm and hands fidget against the bed. It wasn't that she didn't want him to. It just somehow felt...*more* than it ever had before.

He leaned back over her, every plane of his body pressed flat against hers, as he pressed a kiss to her lips. Hard and deep enough that it drove the thoughts a little farther away.

But still.

Seeming to sense it, Miller pulled back. "We can stop—if it's too—"

"It's okay," she breathed. "I just—I just got a little nervous, I guess."

A small, shy smile crossed his face. "Me too."

"Okay." She readjusted herself on the pillow and gripped his shoulders. "Just don't make fun of me if I start laughing."

"Laughing?"

A small laugh squeezed out, and she covered her mouth with her hand. "Oh, God. Like that." Now that she'd started, the floodgates had opened. She giggled again.

"Nervous." Laugh. "Laughter." Laugh. "Oh, God."

Miller leaned back on his knees and looked down at her with a wide grin as she clamped a hand over her mouth in a pathetic attempt to control it. He leaned down, took her face in both hands, and kissed her again, gently this time.

"Jo, that's the cutest fucking thing I've ever seen."

He trailed his lips down her jaw, to her neck, her chest. "But I appreciate the warning." He reached her stomach, his tongue tracing lightly along her skin, until he reached her hips. "Because at least I know you aren't laughing at me."

She let out a shuddering breath and stared up at the ceiling as he hooked a hand under her knee and pulled her leg over his shoulder. And suddenly, she didn't feel like laughing anymore.

15

FRESHMAN YEAR - DECEMBER

"YOU *PROMISED*," JO COMPLAINED.

Miller hesitated outside the door, looking at the room like he was walking into an execution. His hands were tightly fisted around his backpack straps, his feet already pointed in the opposite direction. Jo grabbed his shirtsleeve and yanked him toward the classroom. It was the first time she'd managed to pull herself out of bed for anything other than class in weeks, and she refused to chicken out now.

"You're coming with me whether you like it or not," she said.

He let out a small groan but allowed her to pull him along, because they both knew she wouldn't have been able to move him if he really didn't want her to. And they also both knew he wasn't nearly as reluctant to be here as he was pretending to be, not when *he'd* been the one to slip the interest flyer under her door.

The classroom was mostly empty when they stepped inside, aside from a petite girl with dark brown skin in the back and an Asian guy with glasses in the front row. Both looked up and beamed at their arrival, something like relief washing over their expressions.

Jo glanced at the clock to double-check if they'd gotten there early, but the meeting was supposed to start in two minutes. The meeting was at a weird time, sure—usually people were still at dinner at seven—but surely this couldn't be the only turnout. Miller glanced at her sideways, clearly not impressed, but she just pointed at some chairs in the middle. Sighing, he slid into one and dropped his backpack on the floor beside him.

Jo was about to turn around and ask the girl if they were in the right place when a man strolled into the room. He was tall, almost as tall as Miller, with inky black hair all the way down to his shoulders. He paused at the whiteboard, hands on his hips, and looked around, his expression stoic. Then his face transformed into a grin so quickly, he looked like a cartoon.

"Great turnout! Welcome to the newspaper interest meeting! I'm Rodney, the editor in chief. I'm going to pass around a paper for you all to write your names, your majors, any positions within the newspaper that you're interested in, and your school email. And I'll list all of the available positions on the board for you to choose from. Unfortunately, our sports editor and our copy editor couldn't make it tonight, but they're excited to meet you all at our first official meeting next week."

As Rodney turned around to list out the remaining positions on the board, Miller kicked Jo under the desk.

"What?" she mouthed.

He raised his eyebrows at her.

Jo pointed at the position Rodney was currently writing on the board. *Photography Director.* Until she'd seen the open position listed on the flier, she hadn't even known a photography director of a newspaper was a *thing*. And since all of her photography clients for her budding business were back in Colorado and she was practically starting from scratch again, this could be a great opportunity—not to mention how it would look on her resume. Maybe it would even be enough to make up for the pitiful turn her grades were taking this semester.

And she just desperately missed using her camera.

Miller's shoulders slumped in defeat and he leaned back in his desk, apparently done complaining for now.

"A lot of our pieces come from outside submissions," Rodney was saying. "But if any of you are writers and are interested in writing a piece, we have a few upcoming events on campus this week. Just a few hundred words for each of them." He sent around another stack of fliers. Jo barely glanced at the papers as she slid one off the top and passed the rest to Miller. Writing was definitely not her forte. As Miller shuffled through the pages, he sucked in a sharp breath.

Jo glanced at him out of the corner of her eye. A vein bulged in his neck as he got up to walk the papers over to the girl in the back. Jo shot him a questioning look as he slid back into his seat. She picked the paper back off her desk. The first few events listed were boring—speakers, a fundraiser for Greek life—but the third item on the list made Jo's heart come to a complete stop in her chest.

Local rising star United Fates *performing at the annual Winter Ball.*

Black crept into the corners of her vision until the entire room was blurry and her hands shook around the page.

She couldn't escape it. She couldn't escape *him.* Everywhere she went, that song was playing. Every time she closed her eyes, she saw herself alone in that bed, on the bathroom floor, or waiting in the doctor's office. How she'd cried into her pillow every night for a week afterwards. How every piece of clothing she owned, the first thing she thought of was the last time she wore it with Grey. She'd had to get rid of the outfit she'd worn to the doctor's office that day all together. Just looking at it made her sick.

And now *this?*

They were coming *here?*

And of course they were going to play that fucking song. A song about *her,* the girl he threw away, but not before he got a song out of her that finally got them on the radio.

Not before he got her to trust him enough to get what he wanted.

By the time the meeting let out, the sun had long-since set, and the campus was quiet. Small puddles lingered on the paths as Miller and Jo headed back to the dorm, the air still smelling of rain. They walked in silence. Jo's entire body was still hot with rage, its hold on her so strong, it was hard to think through the fog it had created in her mind.

As Jo turned for the steps leading down to their dorm, Miller caught her arm and pulled her to a stop.

She glanced at him over her shoulder. "What?"

He nodded toward the building they'd just passed. "Hold on. I want to show you something."

"Miller," she sighed. "I just want to go home."

"Hey, I just gave you an hour of my life. You can give me five minutes of yours."

She threw her head back and let out a groan, but followed him back toward the building. "It's probably locked," she muttered.

"You're right," he said simply, but his pace didn't falter. He slipped something out of his pocket as they reached the looming red doors to the gym.

"Why the hell do you have a key?" she asked.

He winked at her over his shoulder and shoved the doors open.

"And why are you taking me to a gym that smells like sweaty boys?" she called, though he'd already left her behind and was halfway across the glossy basketball court. She glanced over her shoulder to make sure they wouldn't get caught before slipping inside and closing the door behind her. "Why are we here?"

Miller threw open a different set of doors at the back of the gym and disappeared into the closet without a word.

"Miller!" she whisper-screamed.

All of the lights were off, and elongated shadows stretched across the floor from the large windows overhead. Miller flipped on the closet's light, adding an orange glow to the room. She was about to call out to him again when he reappeared through the doorway, his arms full of black equipment.

"Put your bag down," he said.

"What is that?"

"You're really bad with directions. Has anyone ever told you that?" He stepped into a pocket of moonlight and held up two sets of boxing gloves.

"You're asking me to punch you?" she asked, incredulous. "I mean, I'm definitely in the mood to right now."

He let out an exasperated sigh as he dropped his backpack to the ground. "Are you really telling me you don't have any anger you want to work out right now?"

She shifted on her feet, gaze trained on the gloves in his hands. "I don't know anything about boxing," she finally said.

A slow grin crept onto his face. "Well, you're in luck, because you're looking at the new group fitness boxing instructor."

Her eyebrows lifted. "I didn't know you applied for that."

He shrugged off his sweatshirt and tossed it aside. "Stop stalling and get over here."

"Well, now I really don't want to do it if you're going to kick my ass."

He pushed a set of gloves into her hands. "Put these on."

She glanced over her shoulder again, half wishing someone *would* catch them in here. But also, the idea of punching something right now was a lot more appealing than she wanted to admit. The thought of *him* coming to her school, singing those lyrics about her in front of her classmates. And worse, having them all sing along. Like she was the punchline, and suddenly everyone else was in on the joke.

She tossed her backpack beside his and yanked the jacket from her shoulders. "I don't even know how to put these things on," she mumbled, struggling to attach the Velcro once both hands were in the gloves.

"Here." Miller reached over and secured the straps for her, then took a step back and held up both of his hands. His pads were different, she realized. Just flat, circular targets. At least she didn't have to worry about his fists flying at her face. "Okay, now give me a punch."

She stared at him.

He rolled his eyes and waved one of the pads at her.

She sighed and brought both hands up to guard her face —at least she knew that much—and threw her right arm forward. It connected with the pad in a pathetic, tiny *smack*. "I don't even know what the proper form for this is."

"So fuck proper form. Just hit me as much as you need to until you feel better."

She halfheartedly threw one punch, then another. "You're not." Punch. "The person." Punch. "I want." Punch. "To hit." Punch.

"That was a good one!"

She clenched her teeth and focused on her breath as she pounded her fists into the pads again and again. The more she punched, the more she got into it. The more her thoughts began to quiet, the more she could forget about the concert, the lyrics, the look on Grey's face the last time she saw him. The choice he'd forced her to make alone.

The cold tone of his voice right before he hung up the phone.

The way he never checked in on her after that.

Not even once.

"Jo, I hope you don't take this the wrong way, but have you thought about going to see the school's counselor to talk about all of this? It might help. She's pretty cool, actually."

Jo stopped mid punch, panting for breath, and let her arms drop. Sweat had started to break out on her forehead. "You've gone to see her?"

Miller shrugged. "Yeah, well, my mom is a psychologist, so she's like a hardcore advocate for therapy. She's had me seeing someone most of my life. I don't know. It's nice sometimes. Just to have someone to talk to. Someone impartial." A flicker of discomfort crossed his features, and he dropped his gaze to the floor. "And I know we haven't really talked about it, but I'm here too, just, if you ever wanted to talk about it."

"I think I like the punching better," she muttered.

He raised the pads again. "Have at it."

"I feel like"—she grunted around punches—"he could have at least changed my name for the song, you know?"

"Definitely."

She focused all of her energy on her right side, punching the same pad again and again. "Or, I don't know, called back at *some point* in the last few months to see what happened to me."

Miller grunted and slid back a step against Jo's punches, but now her vision was tinted red, and she didn't think she could stop even if she wanted to. Her knuckles ached with each blow against the pad, but that only made her want to punch harder. The pain flared up her wrist, her forearm, her bicep. It was mesmerizing, in a way, to feel the pain somewhere else for a change.

"Jo—"

At some point she must have started crying. She could feel the hot tears on her cheeks now, but her entire body felt numb, detached. The pain was grounding. The pain was all that was left.

"Then to have the nerve to come here," she growled. "He probably didn't even notice it. Probably doesn't even remember that I'm here. Probably doesn't even remember me at all—"

"*Jo*—" Miller dodged to the side, dropped his pads, and caught her before she could pitch forward as her fist caught air. Her feet tangled with his, and then they were both falling. His hands clamped around her forearms, and her breath caught in her throat as Miller hit the floor on his back and she collapsed on top of him. She felt his breath leave his body as she struggled to catch her own. The tears were freely streaming down her face now, and she hiccuped as Miller's hand came up to cup the back of her head, holding her against his chest. She fisted her hands in his shirt, the sound of his labored breath filling her head.

They laid there like that until both of their breathing returned to normal, and Jo's fingers started to cramp around his shirt.

She pushed up onto her elbows to look at him. He stared back at her, blue eyes wide, lips slightly parted.

"Can we go watch shitty scary movies and get drunk now?" she asked.

He laughed quietly. "Absolutely."

"Did you pick a movie yet?" Jo called from the bathroom. She leaned over the counter and twisted her mouth down so she could finish applying the face mask around her nose. When she was done, she rinsed the last of the paste from her fingers and adjusted the thick, pink headband so none of it would get in her hair.

As she headed back to her room, the door to the suite opened, and Liv and Addie swept in, arms full of shiny new shopping bags.

"Oh," said Addie. "Hi, Jo."

"Nice face mask," added Liv.

The two shared a look, erupted in a fit of giggles, and quickly disappeared into their room, closing the door behind them.

Jo let out a slow breath through her nose. She wasn't going to let them get to her today. She'd stopped bothering trying to be friends with them months ago when she real-ized they were never going to stop making her the punchline to their jokes—disguised under fake smiles and compliments, of course.

"Are you thinking a rewatch or something new?" called Miller. His eyes went wide as she stepped around the corner. "*What* is on your face?"

Jo scooped the bottle of wine off the dresser as she passed and shrugged. "It's charcoal. It cleans your pores."

Miller was sprawled out on her bed, head propped up on her pillows, scrolling through the movies on her TV. He tossed the remote aside and sat up. "You look like you just fell into a mud pit."

"Are you jealous? Do you want one too?"

"Hell yeah, I want one!"

She tossed him a baby blue headband. "You're gonna have to put that on."

When she stepped back into the bedroom, bottle of face mask in hand, Miller was perched on the edge of the bed, his wavy brown hair sticking straight up with the headband. Jo pressed her lips together to keep from laughing and stood in front of him.

"Close your eyes."

He complied, and she smeared the paste on his forehead.

"It's cold," he complained.

"Beauty is pain."

He squinted a single eye open. "How long does it have to stay on?"

"Would you quit talking! If you keep moving, it's gonna end up in your mouth."

"There's a dirty joke in there somewhere," Miller

muttered as she moved on to applying the mask to his nose.

"It usually dries in about ten to fifteen minutes. When it's hard and you can barely move your face, that's when you wash it off." She pulled away and flipped the cap shut with a satisfying *snap*.

Miller opened his eyes and grinned. "How do I look?"

"Like you just fell in a mud pit," she said flatly.

"But I pull it off, right?"

Before Jo could respond, Addie and Liv started blaring music next door, the volume so loud it made their shared wall vibrate. Miller's head whipped around as the lyrics to "Johanna" echoed through the suite. Jo sighed and set the bottle on her desk. Whatever Miller saw on her face made his features harden, wrinkling the face mask, and he jumped up from the bed.

"Don't." She grabbed his wrist before he could storm from the room. "Don't say anything. That's just what they want."

He looked at her incredulously. "They do this often?"

Jo gritted her teeth, picked the remote back up to shift through the movies, and focused on the screen. It happened so often it probably shouldn't have affected her anymore, but each time those lyrics played, it was like hearing them for the first time all over again. Nausea immediately twisted her stomach, bringing her right back to the night in that empty apartment, to laying on that cold bed in the doctor's office.

The song cut off midway, replaced with Liv and Addie's laughter as they stumbled back out of their room and into the hall, slamming the door to the suite shut behind them.

"Seriously, what is wrong with them?" Miller demanded.

"They think they're funny," Jo said flatly, then glanced at Miller's phone as it buzzed against the bed, a Snapchat notification from *Alice* flashing across the screen.

Jo raised her eyebrows, as much as she could among the hardening face mask, grateful for the change in subject. "*Oooooh*, who's Alice? Does she go here?" Jo grabbed the phone and held it out to him.

Miller stared at her for a moment, but seeming to sense she didn't want to talk about it, he let the subject drop. Jo glanced over his shoulder as he opened the snapchat. A girl's face flashed on the screen—chubby cheeks, freckles, braces. She looked about ten years old. "My kid sister," Miller explained.

"What?" Jo squinted at the picture before it disappeared, trying to find the resemblance. It wasn't immediately apparent like it was with some siblings, but if you knew where to look, it was there. The dark hair, obviously. And they both had defined jaw lines. The eyes were what really gave it away though—dark blue and enviably big. "How did I not even know you had a sister?"

"It's not like you've been super forthcoming about your family, either." Miller held up the phone so they could both fit in the picture, him with his tongue stuck out and Jo with her still-grubby fingers from the face mask up in a peace sign.

"You have any secret siblings I should know about?" Miller asked.

"Nope. I'm the one and only." She paused in the bathroom, staring at her reflection, the echoes of the song still lingering in her head. She'd be lying to herself if she said the disappointment didn't hurt just as much. Not just with what happened with Grey, but Addie and Liv too. She'd spent the first few months here so hopeful, so optimistic and surrounded by possibilities—a new boy, new friends. And yet, somehow, it had all managed to go up in smoke before she'd even realized anything was burning.

Miller, however, was a happy surprise. At least she had that much.

She returned to the room and flopped onto the bed on her stomach. Miller leaned over to pour the two glasses of wine on her desk and handed one to her. She propped her feet in his lap as they settled in, Miller poking a finger against his cheek to test the face mask.

"I can't move my forehead," he said.

"That means it's working."

"Can I ask you a serious question?"

Jo glanced at him out of the corner of her eye. "I absolutely cannot take you seriously like this, but go ahead."

"What are your parents like?"

Jo leaned her head back and swirled the wine around in her glass. The only word she could think to describe them was: "Busy."

Miller looked at her. "Busy?"

She shrugged and tried to take a sip of wine, even though her mouth was at ten percent function now. "My dad's a pilot, and my mom's a flight attendant, so they travel a lot. They have my whole life. They've just never really been...around much."

"I'm sorry," Miller said after a beat.

"Sorry?"

He shrugged. "It just sounds...lonely, I guess."

Jo cleared her throat and set her wine back on the nightstand. "I'm gonna go rinse this off." She gestured to her face mask and headed for the bathroom. "Yours looks about ready, too."

She splashed warm water on her face until she could move her muscles again.

"Hurry up!" Miller called. "I'm gonna start the movie!"

Jo padded a towel against her neck and headed back into the bedroom. "You are mighty impatient tonight."

Miller snorted. "Since when do you say *mighty*?"

Jo waved a finger toward him. "You planning on keeping that on all night?"

He tossed her the remote as the opening music started to play, and disappeared into the bathroom. Jo snuggled into her side of the bed, holding her glass of wine to her chest, when Miller's phone buzzed again. Jo scooped it off the blankets.

"Alice responded!"

Miller reappeared and plopped onto the bed hard enough that Jo nearly spilled her wine. "What'd she say?"

Jo opened the snapchat so they could both see the screen. Alice's face reappeared so close to the camera it cut off her chin and forehead. A line of text slashed across her face like a mustache. *She's pretty. You should date her.*

Jo snorted and tossed Miller the phone. "She should see me without the mud-face."

Miller turned the phone toward Jo and snapped another picture, his fingers flying across the screen as he typed.

"What are you saying?" Jo demanded. By the time she leaned over to see the screen, he'd already sent the reply. "You didn't even let me see the picture. Rude."

Miller shrugged innocently and leaned back against the pillows. "Are you actually going to watch the movie, or are you going to ask me what's happening ten minutes in?"

Jo huffed and burrowed farther under the blankets. "Probably both," she muttered.

✦ 16 ✦

SENIOR YEAR - MARCH

JO SQUINTED AGAINST THE LIGHT PEEKING THROUGH THE cracks in her curtains. Usually she was better at remembering to close those before she went to bed. She yawned, rolled onto her back, and rubbed the sleep from her eyes. Judging by the intensity of the light coming through the window, it was late morning. A boneless, contented warmth filled her body as she stretched, and she laid there smiling at the ceiling for a few seconds, still halfway in a dream state. She hadn't slept that well in a *long* time. She rolled over and ran a hand over the empty sheets beside her.

Reality washed over her like ice water, and the night before crashed into her with so much intensity, it momentarily stole her breath.

Oh, God.

Oh, *God.*

She shoved herself into a sitting position, her breaths coming in hard and fast. Now that the images of last night had started playing in her head, she couldn't get them to stop. Miller's hand twisting with hers against the sheets, his teeth grazing her shoulder, his breath in her ear, the feel of his back muscles moving beneath her hands—

She swallowed hard against the feeling rising in her throat, her entire body trembling now.

Miller's clothes were no longer on the floor, and the bedroom door was shut.

The tightness in the back of her throat spread, more images ramming into her mind on a never-ending loop. Looking down at him with her hands pressed to his chest, her name sounding so differently in his voice when it was rough and breathless. Unbidden, another image shoved its way into her brain, a night she thought she'd pushed from her memory all together.

Sitting in that empty apartment, sheets pressed to her chest, staring at the door after Grey had left.

She threw the covers back and stalked over to the closet, pulling out a band T-shirt and a pair of jean shorts. Her hands shook as she stepped over her dress at the foot of the bed and leaned down to look in the mirror over her dresser. Mascara was smeared beneath one eye, but other than that, she actually looked better than she did most mornings. She stared at her reflection, and the eyes that looked back at her were glassy, unfocused. Her lips were a little swollen, and there was the trace of a hickey near her collarbone.

What had she done?

And the question she didn't even want to let form.

Why wasn't he here?

Probably because he'd woken up and felt exactly what she was feeling right now.

Last night felt dreamy, distant. The logic and common sense abiding by another set of rules. But everything always looked different in the morning.

This never should've happened. *How* did this happen? Miller was...*Miller.* Her best friend. She couldn't lose that over this. She *couldn't.*

Her phone *dinged* on the dresser. A text from Gracie appeared.

Sorry, I might be running a bit late. I just finished packing up all the supplies. Be there soon!

Her eyes darted to the date, then the time.

"Shit."

She yanked the bedroom door open—the only thing that would make her feel better right now was a very large, very strong cup of coffee. And now she was going to have to drink it on the go. The second she stepped into the hallway, her front door opened.

She froze as Miller ducked through the door, his shoulders dark with rain. He was in a gray sweatshirt and black shorts, so he must have gone downstairs to change at some point. He glanced up and noticed her staring at him and smiled, raising two cups of coffee and a small, brown paper bag. "I noticed you were out of coffee, so I ran down the street. Sorry, I was hoping I could slip back in before you woke up."

She didn't—couldn't—respond.

He came back.

And he was...smiling.

"Hey." He kicked the door shut behind him and paced into the kitchen, shooting a second, searching glance in her direction. "You okay?"

"Yeah. Yeah. Of course." She cleared her throat and dropped her gaze. "That coffee smells really good, but I actually have to go."

"Go?" he repeated.

She hurried over to the entryway and slipped on the first pair of shoes she could find, then wrestled around in the coat closet for her camera equipment. "I have a shoot this morning. I completely forgot. Gracie is tagging along for mentoring too..." She yanked the last of her equipment out of the closet and threw the bag over her shoulder. "And I'm supposed to meet her in..." She glanced down at her watch. "Fuck. Five minutes."

"Oh, shit." He held the coffee toward her. "You want me to give you a ride?"

"No, no," she insisted, her voice coming out way too high as she accepted the coffee. "I've got it." She paused by the door, slightly out of breath. "I'm really sorry to run out like this, but I really have to..." She jabbed her thumb over her shoulder. "But you should"—she waved her arm around, not quite sure what she gesturing to—"stay...and... eat that...and...I'll see you later?"

He leaned back against the counter, his expression unreadable. "No, it's cool. Go ahead."

"Cool," she repeated, then turned and all but ran from the apartment. The second the door closed between them, she collapsed against it, panting and trying to catch her breath.

"Could you have made that any more fucking weird?" she muttered to herself.

Her phone *dinged* with another message from Gracie.

Almost there!

"Fuck." She readjusted the bag on her shoulder and hurried off down the hall, making it all the way to her car before she realized she hadn't even remembered to put on a bra.

ON THE BRIGHT SIDE, THE RAIN FINALLY LET UP AS JO pulled her car into campus, the sun coming down prettily through the parting clouds and glimmering off the wet sidewalks. It wasn't the ideal day for photos, but she didn't have any room left in her calendar to reschedule the shoot, so if the girls wanted the pictures, it had to be today. Not that she would mind if these particular clients decided to cancel.

Gracie momentarily blocked out the sun from Jo's vantage point on the ground as she trekked toward her from the opposite direction, carrying a duffle bag half her size.

"I think this is everything!" she called.

Jo finally chose which lens she wanted to start with and attached it to her camera. She felt better now with it in her hands—something familiar, concrete. It wouldn't be enough to erase or forget what had happened last night, but it might be enough to distract her for a while. "Careful with that!" she called.

Gracie was out of breath by the time she reached her, and she gingerly set the bag in the grass. Glass clanged around on the inside. Gracie set her hands on her hips, her curly blonde hair in a tight ponytail today. In fact, her entire ensemble looked like she was prepared for manual labor—running shorts, tennis shoes, an old T-shirt with paint stains.

Jo checked the time on her phone and slipped a freshly charged battery into her camera. "Thanks again for doing this, Gracie. It's going to be a lot to juggle today."

Gracie perked up. "Thanks for letting me! Should I start getting the stuff out?" She jabbed her thumb toward the monstrous bag.

Jo nodded, checking the note on her phone again. "Amber is first, and I think she wants the confetti, a champagne bottle, and she's bringing a few other things with her."

Gracie nodded and knelt to dig through the bag until she found the right props. "How many girls are we doing today?" she asked.

"Five," said Jo. "They're all sorority sisters, so they wanted a couple of shots together, but we're going to start with the one-on-ones, just in case we run out of time. Oh, also, get out the message board. I think all of them wanted to use it."

Gracie quickly assembled the necessary props and pulled two water bottles out of the bag, offering one to Jo. Jo set hers off to the side and scrolled to the oldest pictures on her memory card to make sure she'd have enough space for today. When she reached the end, the photo that popped onto the screen made her breath catch in her throat.

It was blurry and had a huge glare in the upper right corner. She must have missed this one the last time she cleared the card. Miller's face took up the majority of the frame, his dimpled smile stretched as far across his face as it could go, guacamole smeared on the tip of his nose. It was from the night of the frat cocktail, the festive lanterns in the Mexican restaurant casting a red tint over the whole photo. His eyes stared straight in the lens, slightly glassy from the booze, but still, it felt like he was looking right at her.

"Jo?" Gracie's face swam into view behind the camera. "You okay?"

Jo quickly clicked out of the preview, the coffee she'd chugged on the way over here churning in her stomach. "Yeah."

The girls all showed up together, each carrying bags with other props or outfit changes. One noticeably stayed behind the rest of the pack, leaving plenty of distance between her and Jo. Jo resisted the urge to roll her eyes. If she couldn't handle being around Jo, then she shouldn't have hired her.

"Hi, Kayleigh," Jo called, forcing the girl to finally look at her. She was in a sleek, white dress and black high heels, her various colored cords strung around her neck and a graduation cap in her hand.

She shifted her weight and finally met Jo's eyes. "Hi, Jo."

If the rest of the girls picked up on the tension between

the former roommates, they didn't show it—or they just didn't care. Jo pointed Amber over to her first location and set up the shot, getting the first few pictures without any props. The other girls circled around as Jo worked, calling out pose suggestions to Amber.

"You should turn away and look over your shoulder!" said one.

"Oooooh, yeah!" they buzzed in agreement.

Gracie scurried in and out of frame with different props and helped direct the girls for better lighting. Jo smiled a little behind her camera. Honestly, the girl was a natural. With proper training and practice, she might end up being even better than Jo was.

They did close-ups and wide shots, threw confetti and popped champagne bottles, held up messages like *thank God that's over* and *future doctor!*—all the typical stuff. They were cute, and the pictures would turn out fine—definitely something the girls would be satisfied with to post on Instagram or send to their moms or whatever. But Jo had shot a million and one of these. At least last week's girl had taken hers at the local college bar. Now *those* had been some interesting pictures.

When it was Kayleigh's turn, they headed over to the field so she should take some pictures with her lacrosse stick. She stood there awkwardly until Gracie scurried forward and helped her pose. Jo got down on one knee and squinted into the camera, when a figure appeared in the background of the shot. She let out a small frustrated huff and waved her hand toward Gracie.

"Can you tell them to get the hell out of the way?"

Gracie jumped up again, ready to be of service, but the figure kept advancing. A moment later, Jordan's face swam into view through the lens.

A full-body groan filled Jo. This was the *last* thing she needed today. She lowered the camera and rose back to her feet, bracing herself for whatever confrontation Jordan was looking for, but he wasn't even looking at her. He crept up behind Kayleigh, threw his arms around her waist, and spun her in a circle. She squealed and laughed until he set her back on her feet and leaned down to kiss her.

Jo quirked an eyebrow, her mouth slightly open.

"Sorry, sorry!" called Kayleigh. "Babe, we're in the middle of something."

"All right, all right. I'm already gone." Jordan held up his hands and stepped back out of the shot. When Jo didn't move, he motioned for her to continue, apparently now determined to be a spectator for the shoot.

Jo sighed and sank into position as Gracie helped Kayleigh get into the right spot. The hairs along the back of Jo's neck prickled like someone was watching her. Probably Jordan.

So he was dating Kayleigh now, so what? She supposed she should've felt relieved.

They finished off the shots with the lacrosse stick and swapped in the shaken-up champagne bottle.

As Gracie helped set up the next shot, instructing Kayleigh how to open it and where to point it, Jo couldn't help herself. She glanced over at Jordan, who, of course, was already looking at her.

As they wrapped up and the girls headed back to their

car, Gracie stuck around to help Jo clean up and collect the rest of the props.

"Do you have plans this afternoon?" Jo asked.

Gracie zipped up the bag and hefted it onto her shoulder. "No, why?"

Jo shrugged as she finished packing up her camera equipment. "You want to come see how I edit these?"

Gracie beamed. "*Yes.*"

They trekked across the field toward the parking lot, and Jo had half the mind to check in with Miller to make sure he wasn't still there. It had been hours though—surely he hadn't just been waiting around for her all this time. Just thinking his name made her heart drop to the pit of her stomach. And once she opened up a conversation with him again, she was worried about where it might go, if she was ready to talk about any of it yet.

"So..." Gracie peeked at Jo sideways. "Any news on that Sandra Simone job?"

Jo whipped toward her. "How'd you know about that?"

A faint blush crept onto Gracie's cheeks. "Sorry. I overheard you and Miller talking before one of the newspaper meetings."

"Oh. Well. Yeah, she offered me a summer internship, actually."

"Are you going to take it?"

"I think so. I have the paperwork all signed and everything. I just haven't..." she trailed off, really not wanting to get into exactly what was causing her hesitation. "I just need to swing by her office and drop it off. I think I'll go tomorrow before the Criminal Justice banquet."

"Criminal justice?" Gracie asked as they reached Jo's car, and she hefted the bag into the back seat.

Jo rolled her eyes as she slid inside and started the car. "Miller's dragging me there, and I owe him a favor."

Gracie paused, her hand around her seatbelt. "You guys go as friends to a lot of things, huh?"

Jo's stomach twisted again. Gracie wasn't wrong. She and Miller *had* gone to lots of things as friends. They'd been each other's default dates to almost everything since freshman year whenever the other didn't have a real date. And that's what this was when Miller first asked her. But that was weeks ago.

That was before last night.

She hadn't thought that far ahead yet.

"Jo?" Gracie asked. "You okay? You seem kind of...off today."

Jo shook her head, snapping herself out of it, and threw the car into reverse. "Yeah, yeah. Of course."

Gracie narrowed her eyes, like she didn't believe Jo for a second, but said nothing. Jo's mind, however, couldn't stop racing the entire drive home.

❧ 17 ❧

FRESHMAN YEAR - DECEMBER

"MAKE SURE TO EMAIL ME ALL OF THE FINAL DOCUMENTS for the issue before midnight tonight," said Rodney as he paced along the whiteboard at the front of the room. "All late submissions shall be gleefully and thoroughly embarrassed at the start of next week's meeting. Now get the fuck out of here." He pounded his pen against the desk like a gavel and saluted the first round of people that headed for the door.

"You still up for studying in the library?" Miller asked as he shoved his papers in his bag.

"I need to stop by the dorm first," said Jo. "I forgot my book."

Miller threw his head back and groaned, but followed Jo down the hall without further complaint. The dorms and the library were on separate ends of campus, but it was a small school, so it only took about five minutes to get there. Winter had already crept into the days, leaving a faint dusting of snow across the grass and an unforgiving chill in the air. Jo huddled in her jacket as they walked, shoulders drawn up to her ears. Miller sauntered along beside her in nothing more than his usual hoodie, though his cheeks were bright red from the cold.

She left him waiting in the hallway as she slid her key in the lock and hurried into her room. All of the lights in the suite were on, but when she poked her head into the room she shared with Kayleigh, no one was there. She snatched the book off her desk and headed back toward the hall, but froze at the sound of voices coming from behind Addie and Liv's door. She wouldn't have thought anything of it, if she hadn't heard her name.

"*Johanna.*"

The tone was mocking, twisting her name into a joke she didn't understand. It was Addie's voice, she was pretty sure.

"A train wreck," said Liv. "Honestly, I almost feel sorry for her. But I feel even more sorry for *you.*"

There was shuffling on the other side of the door, and then: "It's a nightmare. And what's worse is, she seemed so normal at first, then she just turned out to be a complete fucking psycho."

Kayleigh.

Jo stumbled back a step as the blood drained from her face. Addie and Liv—that wasn't surprising. But hearing the edge to Kayleigh's voice made her ears sting with heat.

"Whatever even happened with that band guy?" asked Addie.

"You've heard the song," laughed Kayleigh. "She was dumb enough to go there, and then he got what he wanted and dumped her like we all knew he would. Then she freaked out."

"Now apparently she's open for business for just about anyone else," muttered Liv.

"Jo, did you find the—" Miller stepped into the room, but froze when he saw her standing there. His eyes flickered from her to Addie and Liv's door. The voices on the other side abruptly cut off, and the handle started to turn, but Jo pivoted and fled into the hall before anyone could open it.

Miller struggled to keep up as Jo speed-walked back across campus, her hands gripping the book so tightly it was starting to hurt. And whatever she'd been feeling before—that awful drop in her stomach, the heat in her cheeks, the shaking in her hands—that was long gone. Now she felt only anger.

Miller finally caught up to her as they reached the quad, and grabbed her shoulder to spin her around to face him. Whatever he saw on her face seemed to stop him in his tracks, however, because he closed his mouth again.

Jo turned wordlessly and glanced both ways before heading across the street to the library. It was mostly empty this time of day, and Jo's steps seemed to echo in the silence as she headed straight for the stairs that led to the private group rooms on the third floor. Miller filed along silently behind her until they reached a room toward the back and closed the door behind them. Jo plopped her bag on the large table in the center of the room.

"Jo?"

She glanced at Miller as he braced his hands on the back of a chair.

"What happened back there?" he asked.

She ripped the zipper of her bag open and started pulling out the contents until a small mountain of books, folders, and papers accumulated in front of her. *Everyone who's pretended to like me the last few months secretly thinks I'm a joke, what else is new?* "Who are you taking to the Winter Ball?" she asked instead.

Miller rocked back on his heels at the change in subject, but hesitated only a moment before shrugging his own bag off and sinking into the chair across from her. "When is that again?"

She shot him a look. "Miller, it's next week."

"Oh." He pulled out a single pen and notebook and shrugged. "I don't think I'm going to go."

Jo reached over and punched him in the arm.

"Ow!" Miller flailed back and cradled his arm to his chest. "What was that for?"

"You're going," was all Jo said as she pulled up a textbook and searched for the assigned chapter.

"I don't get what the big deal is," he muttered.

"Well, I don't either," Jo admitted. "*But* that's why I want to go. I was talking to some of the seniors in photography club, and apparently *everyone* goes. There's all this free food and music, and they do giveaways all night, so there's all these prizes. I heard they literally give away brand new laptops and things like that."

"Great, so you'll go, then report back and tell me how it was."

"*Miller*—"

He pushed his chair back so he was out of reach. "Don't punch me again."

She sighed. "What's it going to take to convince you to go? What if I do everything for you? I'll even find you a date."

"Who's *your* date?" He raised his eyebrows.

She frowned. "Okay, admittedly, I don't have one yet. But I'm *going* to get one."

It's not like she could go with Kayleigh, Liv, and Addie as a girls' group anymore. The thought of faking smiles and playing nice now that she knew what they really thought of her made the nausea surge up in her stomach again. And she couldn't just *not* go now, because that would be letting them win.

It would be like letting Grey win, because she'd be lying if she said a part of her didn't want to skip the whole thing just so she wouldn't have to see him. But no, she wouldn't let him ruin this for her.

She had to go, and she had to find a date.

Miller sighed. "You're going to be working all night anyway, so what do you need a date for?"

"I'm taking pictures for the newspaper—it's not like it's going to take all night. Rodney even told me not to get too swept up in it and still have a good time. They just need a couple of good shots. So what am I supposed to do the rest of the time I'm there when I'm not taking pictures? Dance with myself?"

Miller shrugged as if this were a perfectly reasonable thing to do.

"You're really telling me there's not a single person you want to ask?"

Miller hesitated, then shook his head.

Jo sighed and flipped the page in her book. "You know what? Never mind. Forget it."

"Oh, come on, Jo. Don't be mad."

She flipped the page again, ignoring him.

Miller leaned forward and grabbed her wrist. "I'll tell you what, you find me a date, and I'll find one for you, then we can all go together."

Her shoulders slumped, and she searched his face for any trace of mocking. "Are you messing with me?"

"I'm serious," he laughed. "I can be serious when I want to be."

"Fine." She narrowed her eyes. "You're not going to purposefully get me the worst date ever, are you?"

"I promise to get you the best date I can find." He held out a hand. "Deal?"

Jo wanted to hesitate, show some kind of reluctance. But she really was short on other options, and for once, her desire to go outweighed her pride. She grabbed his hand and gave it a firm shake across the table. "Deal."

THE LINE TO GET INTO THE BALL WAS LONG, PRACTICALLY stretching across the back quad as the faculty at the front checked tickets and IDs. Jo shivered in her trench coat, which was unfortunately much more fashionable than it was functional. Beneath it, she wore a thin silk dress that did little to counteract the cold. Her hair was pinned up in an intricate bun on the top of her head, leaving the back of her neck exposed, but showing off her earrings—a thin silver cord with a single ball on each end.

Her date, Felix, smiled at her as he shoved his hands in his suit pockets and blew out a breath that puffed up in a cloud in front of him. He was a friend of Miller's from the English department, and was barely taller than Jo in her high heels. He had dark brown skin and round, boyish cheeks that dimpled around his smiles. He seemed nice though, if a little nervous. He had Jo's camera bag slung over his shoulder and a flask stashed in the inside pocket of his jacket for later.

"This line isn't moving at all, and it's freezing out here," complained Shay behind them—Miller's date. She shifted her weight back and forth in her dizzyingly tall heels that were a perfect match to her red dress. At least hers had long sleeves. She had a full-on winter coat, too.

Jo bit back her annoyance, especially considering *she* was the one who'd cornered Shay on her way out of the library that afternoon and convinced her to go with Miller. She was pretty, Jo supposed, in the classic sort of way. Big eyes, lightly bronzed skin, long, blonde hair. She was also a sophomore, but apparently didn't mind hanging out with a bunch of freshmen. She was comically short next to Miller, who had his suit jacket unbuttoned and his head craned back toward the sky, looking at the stars as if the cold didn't bother him at all.

Colored lights flashed in the windows as they inched closer to the building, music spilling out the open door. Each floor held a different attraction—the top floor housing the largest of the ball rooms, so it held the band and a large dance floor. The middle level was full of activities like tarot readings and poker tables. The basement held most of the food and places to enter the different giveaways for the night.

Felix glanced at Jo as they finally made it inside and dropped their coats off at the coat check. "Where to first?" he asked.

Jo glanced around, considering. They'd purposefully stayed at their pregame long enough to make them fashionably late, so the crowd was already thick. She slipped her camera out of her bag and double-checked the settings as Miller and Shay reappeared.

"You guys go ahead," Jo told them. "I'm going to make some rounds." She held up the camera.

Miller opened his mouth to say something, but Shay grabbed his arm and chirped out a quick, *"Great!"* before he had the chance. Then she was pulling him toward the staircase at the back to head to a different floor.

"I won't be offended if you ditch me too," she told Felix.

"Nah, you're my date. And I don't mind. I think it's kind of cool."

Jo glanced around the lobby—rounded with bright red decorations and twinkly lights. The overhang from the floors above were visible if you craned your neck back, and they all appeared to be just as busy as the first floor. She eyed the small bar by the coat check, wishing she could grab something despite the lingering heat in her stomach from downing a bunch of shots at the pregame. "We can go floor by floor," she finally said. "And work our way up?"

Felix gestured for her to lead the way. "You're the boss."

Jo started with shots of the building itself, making sure to catch the decorations and colorful lanterns along the ceiling. The moment people saw the camera, they transformed—posing, smiling, and in one case, hiding the flask they'd been trying to sneak a sip from.

Groups hurried past them, all donning suits and sparkling gowns, the majority of which were floor-length. Jo glanced down at her own dress, thankful she'd decided on the mid-calf one instead of the mid-thigh. Even the professors mingling about were fully decked out, sipping champagne and laughing with each other. Felix followed her around dutifully as she grabbed some pictures of people entering, a full-room shot, and one angled toward the domed roof to show the strings of lights around the railing on each floor's overhang.

They did the same thing on the second floor, which had a much darker color scheme than the first. This one was all blacks, purples, and whites. A projector was set up in the corner to cast a galaxy of stars on the ceiling. In the center of the room, there was a large booth where a woman was reading palms and telling fortunes. Jo grabbed a few shots as a couple sat down for a reading.

She was about to turn and carry on when Felix caught her wrist and nodded at the now-open seats. "Come on. I want to know what my future holds."

The woman flashed a yellow-toothed smile at them as they sank into the seats, then aggressively shuffled the cards over the table. Felix waved for Jo to hand over the camera. She narrowed her eyes at him, but obliged, and he stood so he could get a good shot of Jo as the woman laid her cards out on the table.

"Oh dear," murmured the woman.

Jo resisted the urge to roll her eyes. "Let me guess. Untimely death? I've been cursed?"

Felix snorted as he fell back into the seat beside her and squinted at the three cards in front of them. Jo had no idea how to read these things, but none of them looked pleasant.

"This here is the ten of swords." The woman pushed the first card toward her. A man was splayed out with the swords protruding from his back, the red paint dripping to the edges of the card like blood. "Could mean an unwelcome surprise is coming to you. Or, maybe something bad has already happened. You've been backstabbed, so to speak, by someone you cared for." Her eyes flicked up to gauge Jo's reaction. Jo swallowed hard and tried not to let it show on her face, despite the violent drop of her stomach and the heat rising into her cheeks.

"Next, we have death." She tapped the next card, where a skeleton figure cloaked in black sat on a horse.

"So it *is* an untimely death then," Jo quipped, though her voice came out flat.

"Most people take this card far too literally," the woman explained. "This could just mean you're nearing the ending of a major phase of your life. If you resist these necessary endings, it oftentimes just causes more pain."

Jo glanced at Felix out of the corner of her eye, and he shrugged.

"This is what I find the most interesting," mused the woman. "Your final card is the tower."

Jo frowned down at the image—there was a tower in the center, but more strikingly was the way it was up in *flames* and bodies were falling out the sides.

"The tower can represent many things. Usually something shocking is going to happen, something out of the blue, that shakes up your status quo."

"So let me get this straight." Jo pointed to the cards and glanced at the woman, silently asking permission. The woman spread her hands wide and leaned back in her chair, her head cocked to the side as if she were studying Jo. Jo slid the cards closer and tapped the first one. "Something bad already happened to me." She pointed to the second. "Whatever is happening in my life now is coming to an end. And finally." She picked up the third card between two fingers. "My entire world is now going to be turned upside down."

The woman nodded solemnly, and the gold beads on her headdress jangled together.

"All right. Cool." Jo patted the table with both hands and stood.

"Sorry about that," Felix muttered under his breath as he hurried after her. "I thought that would be a lot more...lighthearted."

She raised her eyebrows at him. "Could've been worse, I guess. She could've told me I was going to die."

He snorted. "I suppose you're right."

The music grew louder as they climbed the stairs to the top floor, where the band was clearly already in full swing. Spotlights swept across the dance floor full of gyrating bodies. Small bar tables lined the periphery of the room, with a buffet and bar set up in the back.

Jo caught sight of a familiar dark head above the masses in the center of the dance floor, the lights glowing around his profile. Miller bobbed around less than enthusiastically as Shay shimmied against him and grabbed his hands, sliding them along her body as she moved.

Felix let out a small snort beside her. "I've seen weirder couples, I guess."

Jo smirked and brought the camera to her eye to take a few shots of some nearby dancers. Once she was satisfied, she pivoted, zoomed in on Miller's grimacing face, and snapped a quick picture. "He's awkward as ever."

She continued to scan the room and froze with her lens trained on a group of girls in the corner. Kayleigh had her head thrown back in a laugh, her blonde curls pinned to the top of her head. She clung to Liv's arm to keep upright as Addie was talking. Jo quickly lowered her camera, the conversation she'd overheard resurfacing in her head. The mocking tone of their voices, twisting her name into something ugly. The way even Kayleigh had joined in. Addie and Liv—she could've expected as much. But with Kayleigh, sure, Jo wasn't always the easiest person to be around, and she knew she wasn't the most drama-free roommate, but they'd had good times together. At least, she'd thought they had.

"Think you've earned a break yet?" Felix jutted his chin toward the dance floor.

The song shifted, and Jo looked up toward the stage. A familiar face peered back from the center of the spotlight, half of his face tinted purple. When his gaze landed on her, a current of electricity ran from her scalp to the tips of her toes, and she sucked in a shallow breath, already turning toward the exit.

She'd known he'd be here. Of course she had. She'd seen the posters plastered all over campus. The article they'd printed in the paper. But still. The idea of it and being in the same room as him again were two very, very different things. The vodka threatened to make a reappearance as she stumbled back a step. Suddenly there wasn't enough air in the room—there wasn't enough air in the *world*. And there certainly wasn't enough space between her and Grey.

She took another step back and ran into someone. "Sorry." She turned and came face to face with Rodney, their newspaper editor. He grinned at her, a petite brunette girl in a red, floor-length dress on his arm.

"Jo! Glad I ran into you. Would you mind heading up near the stage and grabbing some close-ups of the band? But then you two should go have fun!" He clapped Jo and Felix on the back, then disappeared onto the dance floor before Jo could respond.

The very idea made her want to throw up. But Jo's hands tightened around the camera as she set her jaw. She could do this. Grey held no power over her, and running out of this room was just letting him win. She had a job to do here, and she had every intention of blowing Rodney away with her work from tonight. She shot Felix an apologetic look and ventured closer to the stage. "I'll be right back," she said over her shoulder.

She slipped to the outskirts of the crowd and came up near the side of the stage, squinting into the camera and zooming her lens, trying to get a shot of the band without a million heads in the way. Twisting, she took a few looking out at the crowd with the band in the foreground. The song shifted again, this time to something slower, and when she turned her camera back to the stage, Grey looked directly at her through the lens and smirked. Her stomach flipped so violently, she thought she might be sick right then and there. But she forced herself to take the picture. It was a good one if you didn't know the story behind it.

As she lowered her camera and pulled her lens cap out of her bag, Grey said into the microphone, "Thanks, everyone. You've been a great crowd! We're gonna take a quick break and be back in fifteen!"

Then he turned and headed toward Jo.

He hopped off the stage and landed directly in front of her before she had the chance to escape. She hadn't known what to expect if she ever saw him again, given how cold he'd been during their last exchange, but she certainly hadn't expected him to smile down at her the way he was, as if nothing had changed.

She stood, frozen, as he laid his hand on her elbow and guided her back, just behind the stage.

"Glad the paparazzi is *finally* taking notice of me."

She shifted her weight to put more space between them. "I work for the school newspaper."

"Well?" He smiled again. "Did you get any good shots of me? Want me to pose for you now?" He tilted his face back and forth, exposing every angle of his profile.

"I should get back to my date."

"Oh! A *date*! What's his name?"

"Grey," she warned.

"*Another* Grey? You certainly have a type, don't you?"

She glared at him.

"What?" He laughed and ran a hand through his hair. "You think a little misunderstanding means we can't be friends?"

She stared at him as her brain slowly processed his words. "A misunderstanding?" she whispered.

"Well, yeah." He gestured toward her stomach. "Clearly you were mistaken, and that's quite all right. It happens."

Mistaken.

She stared at him. She stared at him for what felt like a very long time, the blood slowing draining from her face, then turned toward the crowd so he couldn't see it. So he couldn't see the nausea threatening to surge up from the pit of her stomach. The anger causing her shaking hands to turn into fists.

The tears springing to the corners of her eyes.

Above the crowd, one tall head was turned in her direction. She met Miller's eyes, just for a second, her vision slightly blurry with tears. She blinked and hurried away from Grey without a word, desperately pushing toward the exit.

"Johanna!" Grey called after her, but she kept moving. She didn't know where she was going. All she knew was she had to get out of here.

Mistaken.

She wished she could crumple up the word and shove it down his throat until he choked on it.

She was nearly to the door when someone caught her elbow and pulled her to a stop. She looked up to see Miller staring down at her, his eyebrows pulled together.

"Are you all right?" he asked. "What did he say?"

"I'm fine." She pulled her arm from his grasp, fingers still trembling. "I'm just gonna go home."

Miller glanced back toward the stage for a moment. "What happened?"

"Nothing. I just—I think I went a little overboard at the pregame," she said, though she'd never felt more sober in her life. "And I already got all of the shots I need for the night."

The concerned expression didn't ease from his face. "You want me to come with you?"

Shay appeared at his side and threw herself around his arm. "*There* you are. Oh, hi, Jo!"

"Hi, Shay," Jo murmured. She swallowed hard and met Miller's gaze. "I'm fine. You stay. I'll see you tomorrow."

"You're *leaving?*" Shay demanded, then turned to Miller. "You can't *leave*. I want to keep dancing."

Miller opened his mouth like he wanted to protest, and Jo glanced between the two of them.

"Stay, really. I'll just see you guys tomorrow."

"Great!" Shay tugged on Miller's arm. "Let's go check out the buffet."

"Tell Felix I'm sorry," said Jo.

"Jo—" Miller called, but she was already out the door.

18

SENIOR YEAR - MARCH

JO STARED AT THE TWO UNANSWERED TEXTS FROM Miller waiting on her phone. Nothing pressing—just asking how the shoot went, if it was weird seeing Kayleigh, that he was excited for tonight. She wasn't ignoring him, per se, but she didn't know how to respond. Her entire body seized up at the thought.

Maybe it was from the conversation with Gracie yesterday, or maybe it was something else. They needed to talk about what happened between them—that was inevitable. But the full weight of that was just now crashing into her.

Pieces of that night kept flashing into her mind unbidden—just fragments and heartbeats. His breath in her ear, his hands in her hair, the heat of his skin. They mingled with the images she was all too familiar with— him sleeping on the floor the night he'd let her sleep in his bed, him rolling his eyes at her from the driver seat when he picked her up from a party, all of the shoulder punches and hugs and touches that hadn't meant anything—that hadn't made her *feel* anything, anything at all.

How could things be so different so suddenly? She couldn't make sense of it. No matter how hard she tried to force the pieces to fit together, they just wouldn't.

And now that their friendship was stained with the new moments, she didn't know if the old ones would ever be possible again. Or if she even wanted them to be.

She sent him a quick, vague text that everything was fine, just so he wouldn't worry. But the weight of everything unsaid between them was so thick in the back of her throat, she felt like choking on it.

She stared at the dress she'd set out for tonight—floorlength and gold with a low back and thin straps. She hadn't decided on the shoes yet, but it could wait. She needed to get out of this damn apartment. Every time she looked at the bed or the wall or the dresser, her mind force-fed her images of what had happened there.

She still needed to drop off her paperwork and pick up her new ID card from Sandra's office. If nothing else, it would kill some time and serve as a much-needed distraction.

She gathered her things, triple-checking the paperwork was in her bag, before slipping out the door and heading down to the lobby. Her footsteps echoed in the empty room, and the door flew open right as she reached it. She stumbled back a step, narrowly avoiding running into the person entering the building.

"Sorry, sorry," he said.

Jo froze at the familiar voice, and when he looked up to meet her gaze, his eyes widened.

"Jo. Hey."

"Hey, Jordan." She stepped aside so he could pass, willing him to keep walking, but of course, he did no such thing.

"Hey, I've actually been meaning to talk to you."

"Oh?" Jo raised her eyebrows. "I was just heading out..."

"Right, right." He stepped away from the door so she could pass, but reached out and lightly brushed his fingertips against her elbow. "I just wanted to apologize for how I acted. Especially at the cocktail. I feel really bad. And that whole thing with Miller's paper—I talked to Wells and got the grade fixed and everything."

Jo waved a hand, slightly startled at the mention of the cocktail. With everything else going on, she'd nearly forgotten about it.

"No, really. I was a dick, and you were never anything but nice to me. The last thing you deserved was another guy treating you like that. I'm sorry."

Jo went still, her stomach clenching at his choice of words before her brain quite caught up to why it had unsettled her. "Another?" she asked.

He shifted his weight, one hand coming to scratch at the back of his neck. "Yeah, I—anyway. Have a good rest of your day, Jo. I'll see you around." He turned toward the elevators, but before he went, Jo could've sworn his eyes had trailed down to her stomach.

～

JO DROVE IN SILENCE, SAVE FOR THE LOW HUM OF THE AC in an attempt to counteract the sun beating through her windshield. She gripped the steering wheel until white split across her knuckles.

Jordan knew. She didn't know how he knew, but he did. She could feel it. Not just from the way he'd looked at her, but as she went back, analyzing every moment of their interaction, everything he'd said, the way he'd stood—he knew about freshman year.

But *how?*

And why now?

He'd never looked at her like that before, so he must have learned recently.

But the only other person who knew what happened was Miller. And she knew Miller. She *trusted* Miller. And in no stretch of the imagination could she see Miller going around and gossiping about the worst thing that had ever happened to her, not after he'd been there. Not when he'd seen what it had done to her. Not after the other night—

But then how had Jordan known? She didn't even know him freshman year. The lines of the road blurred in front of her as her GPS barked off directions that she couldn't hear over the roar in her ears. Her brain desperately searched for a reasonable explanation.

The parking lot across from Sandra Simone's office was nearly full when Jo pulled in. The sun reflected off the buildings as Jo climbed out of her car, sucking in as many deep breaths as she could as if she could cleanse the last hour from her system. She paused on the sidewalk, threw her shoulders back, and strode inside.

Brenda, the receptionist, smiled at her. "Hi, Jo!"

"Hey." She pulled the papers out of her bag. "I'm here to drop these off? And I think I'm supposed to pick something up, too."

"Of course! Go ahead and grab a seat. She'll be right out."

Jo grabbed one of the mints from the coffee table and popped it in her mouth as she sunk into the plush chair in the corner. Her phone buzzed with another text from Miller, but she didn't open it. Seeing his name on her phone made her chest clench and a million things she didn't want to think about right now spiral through her mind.

She heard Sandra's high heels before she saw her, and oddly enough, a second pair of footsteps. Jo didn't even have the chance to venture a guess as to who else would be here before Sandra and her visitor rounded the corner.

Grey.

Her heart came to a complete stop in her chest.

Grey paused at the front desk, watching her, as Sandra continued forward, arms spread wide like she was going in for a hug, but Jo barely felt it as the woman's arms squeezed her.

Jo held up the papers between them, forcing a smile onto her face, despite every inch of her skin burning as she felt Grey's gaze on her.

The last time she'd seen him was the Winter Ball freshman year—and she'd kind of assumed that would be the last time ever, especially after he'd moved to LA. And even though many things had changed in the last four years, and the wounds weren't nearly as deep or tender as they'd been back then, still, seeing him, being in the same room as him, it was like someone had dumped ice cold water over her head.

"Oh!" Sandra stepped to the side and motioned Grey over. "Johanna, this is my son, Grey. Grey, this is Johanna. She's going to be our new intern this summer."

Grey didn't hesitate before stepping forward and offering his hand to shake. "Nice to meet you, Johanna."

The last thing Jo wanted to do was touch him, but she shook his hand, and he gave her a knowing smile. God, she hated that smile. But more than anything, she hated the small flash of gratitude she felt that he was pretending he didn't know her. That would've prompted a whole awkward conversation on why Jo hadn't told Sandra that first day that she knew her son.

Brenda appeared and handed Jo her ID card that would let her in the employee entrance in the back as Sandra confirmed Jo's start day—two days after graduation.

"I'm really sorry to rush out," said Jo. "But I have this thing tonight."

The fact that her *thing* was more than five hours from now didn't really seem like necessary information to share.

"I'll walk you out," offered Grey.

"It was nice to see you, Jo!" called Brenda.

Jo waved as she hurried out the door, pointedly not looking at Grey as he followed her.

"Johanna Palmer," he said once they were alone on the sidewalk.

"I didn't know she was your mom."

Grey shrugged. "I know. She told me she pursued you. Showed me your portfolio and everything. I'll admit, I was impressed."

"Cool. I'm leaving now." Jo glanced both ways down the street, waiting for a line of cars to pass.

"Johanna—"

"*Don't* call me that."

He let out a startled laugh. "Is that not your name?"

"Everyone just calls me Jo." *You were the only one who ever called me Johanna*, was what she didn't say.

I can't stand for anyone else to call me that anymore, was what she couldn't say.

"Jo." Grey stepped up next to her on the curb. "Let me buy you a cup of coffee."

"No."

"Jo—"

"What the hell do you want from me?" she demanded, finally turning to face him.

The arrogant smile finally fell from his face, and he paused a moment before responding. "I want to buy you a cup of coffee. And I want to apologize." She opened her mouth to protest again, and he seemed to sense it, because he continued before she had the chance. "I know I don't deserve it. But I'm asking you for five minutes of your time. You can even throw the coffee on me afterwards, if you want."

Jo snorted at that, but her chest warmed a little at the visual.

"Please, Jo," he added quietly. "I just want to talk."

She glanced back at the street, now empty and ready

for her to cross. But her feet didn't move. She'd always thought she didn't want anything from Grey anymore—and for the most part, that was true. But she'd also thought she'd never see him again. She'd thought he was frozen in time as the boy she'd known when she was eighteen. But this person standing beside her didn't look quite like him. He was heavier now and clean-shaven for once. But there was also something different about his eyes. The way he looked at her. The way she actually believed him when he said he wanted to apologize, something she'd stopped waiting for years ago.

"Whatever you have to say, just spit it out." She stared at him, waiting for him to continue. Now that the initial shock of seeing him had filtered out, Jo was pleased to realize she didn't feel much of anything when she looked at him anymore. Not attraction. Not desire. Not heartache. Not even anger. He was just...there. A version of a person she didn't know.

"All right." He cleared his throat and shoved his hands in his pockets, his usual confidence and ease strikingly absent. "I'm not here to give you excuses or to ask for your forgiveness. I've thought about reaching out so many times —after you launched your new business, when I saw that piece on you in the paper—and I talked myself out of it every time."

Jo bristled a bit. "You've been keeping tabs on me?"

He shrugged. "I—look, I'm sorry. I was a stupid kid—"

"You were twenty-two," she cut in. "That's how old I am now. So no, you weren't a kid."

"You're right," he said quietly. "The way I handled that

is the worst thing I've ever done. It's not an excuse, but I was *scared*, Jo. After I hung up the phone with you, I threw up."

Her jaw tightened. "And then you got to forget about it, go on with your life, and tour the world."

"I never forgot about it," he whispered. "But you're right. I don't think there was a worse way I could've done things. I'm sorry. I'm sorry that I hurt you. I'm just—I need you to know that."

Jo squinted and turned away to look across the street as Grey's shoulders slumped pitifully—this boy who had once been larger than life to her, who'd had a magnetic pull she couldn't resist no matter how hard she tried. The first boy she'd ever been in love with. Now she hardly recognized him. And what was probably the most merciful thing about it all was she didn't want to.

"Is that all, then?" she asked.

He looked up, bit his lip, and nodded.

"Okay." Without another word, she turned around and walked away from Grey for the last time.

19

FRESHMAN YEAR - DECEMBER

KAYLEIGH STOOD IN THE DOOR TO THEIR ROOM WITH A rolling suitcase half her size. She pulled on a bright red hat with a pompom on top and glanced back at where Jo was sitting on her bed. A small frown crossed her face. "You sure you're going to be okay here all alone?" she asked. "It's a long break." She hesitated, eyes darting from her suitcase to Jo. "You could always come home with me."

"I'm good. Really." Jo smiled at the offer, even though Kayleigh hadn't meant it. If she had, she would've asked before she was literally walking out the door. "Have fun with your family."

Kayleigh smiled again, looking almost relieved, and gave a halfhearted wave. "Merry Christmas."

Jo waved back, but Kayleigh had already slipped into the hall and closed the door behind her.

Addie and Liv's music pulsed next door, so they, unfortunately, had not left yet. Jo shuffled across the hall in her slippers and sweatpants to knock on Miller's door before they had the chance to realize *she* was still there. He appeared almost immediately, hair standing straight up and a black pair of glasses she'd never seen before propped on his nose.

"Can I hide in here until they leave?" she asked.

He opened the door wider, apparently needing no clarification on who *they* were.

His roommate's bed was neatly made for once, the surrounding shelves slightly cleared out—Alan must have already left. On Miller's side, however, there wasn't a single suitcase or bag in sight.

"Have you not even started packing yet?" Jo demanded.

"Oh yeah." Miller sank into his desk chair and threw a chip in his mouth. "I decided to stay here. My mom's going to some conference, my sister's going to a friend's—just saw no reason to go home, you know? What about you? Need a ride to the airport?"

She hopped onto his bed and crossed her legs beneath her. "Actually, I'm staying too. Both of my parents are working."

He tilted his head to the side, a slow smile spreading across his lips. "Palmer, we get to have Christmas together!"

She let her jaw drop in mock surprise. "Shit. Do I have to get you a present now?"

He pointed at her. "It better be a good one, too. Hey"—he snapped his fingers, his face brightening—"you wanna go get a tree?"

She laughed and leaned back against the wall.

"I'm serious! Just one of those four-foot ones."

"Right now?" she asked in disbelief.

"Hell yeah." He jumped up and grabbed his keys. "I'll drive."

"Miller! I can't go like this." She gestured down to her sweats and slippers.

He widened his eyes and waved at his own sweats, then grabbed her hand and pulled her out the door, pointedly ignoring her protests.

Which was how she found herself in a Target in little more than glamorized pajamas on a Friday night. Luckily, the store was mostly empty, the floors littered with glitter and pine needles—casualties of last-minute Christmas shopping. Miller beelined straight for the Christmas section in the back, and Jo couldn't help but smile as he crouched down to inspect the smaller trees. There were only a few boxes remaining behind the ones on display, making their options pretty limited.

"Green or white?" he asked.

Jo pointed to the one at the end of the line. "Black."

He quirked an eyebrow at her over his shoulder, but slid one of the black boxes off the shelf and tucked it beneath his arm. "Ornaments?"

She gestured for him to lead the way. This aisle was mostly cleared out too, leaving behind little more than random letters and balls covered with glitter. She frowned at their options as Miller ventured farther down the aisle.

"Jo!"

Her head popped up as Miller pulled something down

and held it out to her—a mini camera. "We have to get it," he said.

"Great." She took the cheap plastic from him and blew the air out of her cheeks. "A tree with only one—oh my God." She grabbed a cartoonish, yellow ornament that was supposedly a pack of French fries.

Miller nodded his approval and continued his perusal of the aisle. After adding a ball with *Oregon* across the front, some reindeer, a gigantic, cloth Rudolph, and a few random dinosaurs, Jo's hands were so full, she didn't think she could carry any more. The tree already had lights attached to it, so at least that was one less thing to find.

"Should we go check out?" she offered.

Miller squinted, considering. "Stay here. I'll be right back." He turned and took off without any explanation.

"Where are you going?" she called after him.

"To get a cart," he said just as he slipped around the corner. "I want to hit the baking section next!"

WITHIN DAYS, THE ENTIRE DORM WAS COVERED IN A FINE layer of sugar. All of the countertops in the kitchen were filled with various sheets of cookies, the sink piled high with the dishes they'd neglected to clean yet. Jo was hopeless when it came to baking, and half of her batches came out burnt, but Miller didn't seem to mind. He even ate one and pretended it tasted good even though Jo had spit hers into the trash can.

They set up the tree on the coffee table in the common

room. The dorm was mostly empty for break, silence filling in the usual buzz of voices and sports games blaring from the TV. There was at least one other student there, though Jo had yet to run into them. Whoever they were, they'd added an angel to the top of the tree.

On Christmas morning, Jo stumbled her way to the kitchen, eyes cracked open just enough to locate the coffee maker. She leaned against the counter and rubbed her eyes as it roared to life, her gaze drifting over to the sad little tree on the table. She didn't bother checking her phone to see if her parents had called—their flight was to somewhere in Asia today, so she had a feeling she might not hear from them at all.

"If you make enough for two, I might let you have some of my pancakes," said Miller as he shuffled into the kitchen, looking nearly as exhausted as she was. It was entirely his fault, of course. Jo would've gone to bed at a reasonable time last night if he hadn't insisted on marathoning all of the horrible slasher movies they could find on Netflix. He was still in the same matching sweats and hoodie, so dark they nearly matched the curls of hair spilling onto his forehead. He ducked down to rifle through the cabinets. The coffee maker let out a series of beeps, and he straightened, arms full of ingredients.

"Do you have a mixing bowl?" he asked.

She jutted her chin at one of the cabinets with her name on it and pulled out a couple of mugs. After watering Miller's down with nearly half the bottle of creamer, she slid the mug across the counter to him.

He took a sip and grinned. "Perfect."

Jo wrapped her hands around her own, letting the warmth soak into her palms. "Glad you like your liquid sugar."

"Life's too short to drink things that don't taste good," he informed her as he plopped a few eggs in the bowl.

She pushed herself onto the counter and crossed her legs, watching as he lit up the stove and starting pouring the mix into perfectly symmetrical pancakes.

He peeked an eye at her. "Are you going to tell me I'm doing these wrong, too?"

"No." She glanced away and sipped her coffee. Truthfully, she was trying to remember the last time someone had made her pancakes. Besides her uncle who babysat her on her ninth birthday, nothing came to mind.

He nodded toward the common room. "You want to go put a bad Christmas movie on or something?"

"I can do that."

The hall quickly filled with the smell of pancakes and syrup as Jo found an old Christmas cartoon and settled into the couch. Miller appeared at her side and handed over a generous stack of pancakes, already thoroughly drenched in syrup.

Jo gasped as she took the plate. "You put peanut butter on them?"

He froze, fork still extended toward her. "Is that bad?"

She quickly snatched the fork and cut off a piece. "It's perfect."

Laughing, he fell into the couch beside her and dug into his own plate as a singing snowman waltzed into the scene in front of them.

"These are amazing," said Jo.

Miller just gave a slight bow of his head and slid something out of his pocket—a small, black box. He set it on the couch between them. "Are we doing presents yet?"

Jo glanced from the box to him, then set her plate on the coffee table so she could pick it up.

When she hesitated, he nodded. "Open it."

Inside was a pair of stunning gold hoop earrings, and clearly not the cheap kind. She looked up at him with wide eyes.

"To replace the ones you lost. Yours were probably better than these—"

She leaned forward and pulled him into a hug. He quickly held his plate out to the side before she could crush it between them. "Thank you," she murmured against his neck. "I can't believe you remembered that. This was really thoughtful."

He shrugged as she pulled away, his cheeks now tinged with the slightest blush.

"But now my present is going to look so lame," she said.

He rolled his eyes and set his somehow already empty plate on the coffee table. Jo slid the small envelope out from under the tree and handed it to him.

A smile brushed his eyes as he slid out the card.

"You said you needed new gloves a while ago," Jo explained. "But I didn't have the first idea of which ones to get you. So I just got you a gift card to that boxing store downtown. Is that lame?"

He reached over and squeezed her knee. "It's perfect. Thank you. Merry Christmas."

"Merry Christmas."

They stared at each other for a moment, until Miller cleared his throat and dropped his gaze, then nodded toward the TV. "Wanna ditch the Christmas stuff and put something scary on instead?"

She laughed and jumped up to grab the remote before he could. "Fine. But I get to pick this time."

❧ 20 ☙

SENIOR YEAR – MARCH

Jo probably needed to go back to therapy. She probably should have months ago—probably never should've stopped going in the first place, considering a busy and stressful schedule was more of a reason to go, not less. She'd been bound to have a breakdown of some sort eventually. Sleeping with her best friend hadn't been the tipping point she'd expected, but it was pretty on par with how the rest of Jo's college experience had gone. At least she'd kept up with the meds.

She spent the rest of the afternoon meditating and practicing breathing exercises she'd picked up from her counselor over the years. When that didn't ward off the incoming panic attacks, she went for a run. God, she hated running. Maybe that was what made it so effective. She was so consumed by her own misery and hatred that there wasn't room left in her head for anything else.

When she stumbled back into her apartment, she was

red-faced, smelly, and limping slightly from a shin splint. The red numbers on the clock glowed accusingly at her from the kitchen, and she pointedly avoided looking at the dress she'd laid out at the foot of her bed as she crossed into the bathroom for a shower.

She hadn't forgotten about the banquet tonight. She'd just been hoping her obligation to go would somehow disappear over the course of the day through sheer force of will.

She took longer in the shower than usual, standing under the spray and staring at the wall in front of her instead of blasting music and singing along. If the hot water burned her skin, she didn't notice it.

Two texts and a missed call from Miller flashed on her phone as she climbed out and wrapped a towel around herself. She sat like that on the edge of her bed, goose bumps rising on her legs, water from her hair dripping down her back, for a long while.

Whatever adrenaline or endorphins she'd been buzzing with after her run were gone, and all that was left was the familiar constricting sensation in the center of her chest. The very thought of attending the banquet tonight—of putting on a dress and a fake smile, socializing with a room full of people she didn't care about and convincing Miller nothing was wrong—it was impossible. The very idea of it ignited a bubbling pit of panic in her stomach.

She pulled out her phone and scrolled past Miller's unread messages until she found her chat with Gracie.

I need a favor.

GRACIE HELD THE DRESS OUT AT ARM'S LENGTH, HER EYES darting from the shimmery fabric to Jo's face. She'd arrived less than twenty minutes after Jo sent the text, slightly out of breath and wide-eyed like an over-eager puppy. The moment Jo had expanded on exactly what *favor* she needed, that eager look devolved into one of sheer terror.

"Jo..." Gracie said. "I don't know about this."

"It'll be fun," Jo insisted.

"Then why don't *you* go? Are you and Miller...fighting or something?

Jo sighed and sank onto the foot of her bed. She tried to think of any reasonable explanation other than the truth. But that was the thing—there was simply no other reason she'd break a promise to Miller. There was no other reason she'd let him down like this. Even if she did manage to spin some kind of story, she had a feeling Gracie would see right through it. And if Gracie actually went through with this for her, the truth was the least she deserved.

"We slept together," Jo admitted.

Gracie's eyes nearly bulged out of her head.

Jo bent her head between her knees and ran her hands through her hair. "That's the first time I've said that out loud. Shit." She blew the air out of her cheeks and looked back up at Gracie. "I'm sorry for putting you in the middle. I just...*can't* go tonight. Everything's just a mess up here right now." She waved her hands around her head, her chest constricting as something occurred to her. "Shit. And you like him, so this was a doubly bad idea. I'm sorry. Just forget it. I'll figure something else out."

"No." Gracie frowned down at the dress in her hands. "I'll go."

"Gracie, you don't have to—"

"No, really. It's okay." She turned toward the floor-length mirror and held the dress up to her body. Not admiring, exactly. The look in her eyes was curious. Calculating. "And I don't have a thing for Miller anymore," she added, a corner of her lips lifting. "I'm not a masochist."

Before Jo could work out what that meant, Gracie slipped into the bathroom and closed the door behind her. Jo stared at her reflection while she waited. She looked pale, paler than usual, her hair frizzy and tangled from letting it air-dry. Dark shadows lined her eyes, and even her eyelids seemed to droop under the weight of it all.

"Are you sure Miller is okay with this?" Gracie called through the door.

She could lie to Gracie, Jo supposed, but she'd find out soon enough if she showed up and Miller had no idea what she was doing there. The door swung open and Gracie stepped out, walking on her tiptoes as she headed for the nude high heels set out by the mirror. Despite Gracie being several inches shorter than Jo was, the gold dress fit her well once she propped herself against the wall and slipped the shoes on.

Gracie glanced at Jo over her shoulder, waiting for an answer to her question.

"I texted him that I'd meet him at the banquet," Jo admitted.

Gracie stared at her. "So you want me to just walk up to him and say *surprise?*"

It was a shitty thing to do, but there was no version where she told him ahead of time that would turn out well. If she told Miller she didn't feel up to coming, he'd want to know why. And the more she tried to hide it from him, the more he'd push and worry, and then he'd do something stupid like skip the banquet to come check on her and make sure she was okay. And not only was the banquet mandatory for everyone in the department to be able to *graduate*, it was also an important networking opportunity.

She wasn't going to ruin that for him. Not by making him miss it, and certainly not by showing up in her current train-wreck form.

Jo's thoughts must have shown on her face, because Gracie's expression softened. "Surprise it is."

Jo waved her hand for Gracie to perch on the bench at the end of the bed as she dug out the curling wand from her dresser. "Loose curls?" she asked.

Gracie nodded and met her eyes in the mirror. "You're going to have to talk to him eventually," she said.

"I know." Jo sighed and licked a finger to press against the barrel and test the heat. They sat in silence as Jo got to work on her hair, curling the pieces away from her face and loosening the curls before they had a chance to cool.

"Do you regret it?" Gracie asked after a while. "Is that why you're avoiding him?"

Jo paused with her fingers still sectioning off Gracie's hair. It was a fair enough question. And maybe that was it.

It was the answer to that very question that had her so unnerved, she'd been nauseous all day.

Because the thing was, the answer should've been yes. Miller was her best friend. The one person she knew she could count on no matter what. And she'd impulsively crossed a line with him that had the potential to ruin everything. A line that couldn't be uncrossed. All for one thoughtless night.

But she didn't regret it. Not even a little bit.

✺ 21 ✺

FRESHMAN YEAR - JANUARY

It took Jo nearly twenty minutes to find the fitness studio. Sure, she'd never been there before and hadn't bothered to look it up, so she was partially to blame, but whose brilliant idea was it to put the fitness studio in the basement of a completely different building than the regular fitness center? She'd meant to get there before the class started, but that was starting to look like a fruitless endeavor. She was out of breath by the time she made it to the door, and she shot a quick glance at the clock as she slipped into the room. The class didn't start for another five minutes, but the room was already packed. She managed to squeeze herself into a spot in the back corner behind a tall, blonde guy and quickly tossed her bag against the back wall. The music switched on and vibrated the speakers overhead.

The people around her all started shuffling their feet and bouncing back and forth. Jo quickly mirrored their movements as she fumbled to put her hair up. She looked up to find Miller grinning at her from across the room. He adjusted the microphone hung over his ear as he shuffled his feet along to the music.

"All right, everyone. Guards up." He raised both fists in front of his face as the music shifted, the beat picking up. "Glad you could all make it to class. You picked a good night to be here." His gaze found Jo again, and he winked. "It's gonna be a hard one."

JO STEADIED HERSELF AGAINST THE BACK WALL AS A RIVER of sweat dripped down the bridge of her nose. Thankfully, the room around her was still loud enough with conversations and people leaving that no one could hear her still desperately sucking in air. The rest of the girls around her practically skipped from the room, seemingly unfazed by Miller's death class. He was still at the front, propping open the door to let in some fresh air since the room was now unbearably hot and humid. He paused and held the door open for some people on their way out, smiling.

"Jo?"

Jo turned, nearly losing her balance as she did so. Her leg muscles were still shaking so badly it was like they'd forgotten how to do their job.

Shay stood a few paces away, her hesitant smile widening when Jo met her eyes. Jo hadn't even noticed her in the class. Shay headed over toward Jo's corner of shame, blonde ponytail bouncing with each step, white sports bra and black leggings still in perfect shape. It looked like she hadn't even broken a sweat. "I thought that was you," she said.

Jo eagerly drank from her water bottle and wiped the sweat from her forehead. "Here in my prime."

Shay's expression glitched, like she wasn't quite sure what to make of this, but then blinked a few times, and the smile returned full force. "Wasn't Miller so good up there?"

"He'd do well in a torture scenario, yes."

Shay stared at him for another moment—his back fully to them now as he talked with a tall guy lingering in the doorway—before turning back to Jo. "It's actually lucky running into you like this," she said. "I've been meaning to talk to you."

Jo raised her eyebrows. "About?"

Shay shifted her weight, her eyes darting to the side, just for a second. "About Miller, actually."

Jo's entire body clenched defensively. Sure, Miller being in a relationship had been weird at first, but Jo had been trying to see whatever he saw in Shay and get along with her. If Shay thought that meant she and Jo were friends now, enough that Jo would take her side over Miller's in whatever was going on, she was sorely mistaken. "Look, Shay, if you're having some kind of relationship problem, I'm probably not the best—"

"It's not that."

"Okay..." Jo waited for her to go on, but she didn't say anything else. "Then what is it?"

"Well." Shay chewed on her lip. "There's no good way to say this, but I hope you can see where I'm coming from, because I'm really not trying to be *that* girl, but...well..." she trailed off, her eyes darting toward Miller at the front of the room again. "I know you two are...close. But you have to understand where I'm coming from as his girl-friend now. It just makes me a little *uncomfortable* having you around all the time, and, like, he tells you the things he should tell me, you know? And we all have these busy schedules, so when we *do* finally have some time together, it would be nice if it could just be...us. We just think it would be best if you could take a few steps back, that's all."

Jo tightened her grip on the wall, her stomach clenching into a knot as heat rushed to her face. She schooled her features, hoping the redness lingering in her cheeks from the workout would cover whatever was happening to her body right now. Shay was right about one thing; Miller *did* have a busy schedule. It was the whole reason she'd come to this awful class in the first place. Besides newspaper meetings and running into each other at the dorm, she'd hardly seen Miller in weeks.

But maybe that wasn't an accident like she'd thought.

She couldn't stop her brain from getting stuck on Shay's choice of words.

We.

"Well." Jo turned to pick up her backpack from the floor so Shay couldn't see her face. "If that's what Miller wants, then he can tell me himself."

"You know he's too nice to go through with it," said Shay. "Look, I'm not trying to be that bitchy girlfriend, but he just feels too bad to say anything, so I told him I would."

Jo paused, swallowing hard, before turning back around. "You guys have talked about this?"

Shay laid a hand on her arm, and it took everything in Jo not to pull away. "I like you, Jo. This is really nothing against you. Please tell me you can understand where I'm coming from."

Jo opened her mouth—to say what, she had absolutely no idea—but then Miller appeared at Shay's side, sporting his usual lopsided grin as he threw an arm around Shay's shoulders and pulled her against him.

"Jo! Didn't expect to see you here. What did you think of the class?"

"You're all superhuman," she murmured, her face suddenly hot again as she watched Shay nestle into his side, still watching Jo as if to say, *see? He chose me.* Jo tightened her fist around her bag. "But I should probably get going. Still have a lot of homework to do."

Miller frowned. "You sure? We were gonna go grab a bite to eat. You should come!"

Jo forced a smile, keeping her gaze anywhere but Shay's face. "Maybe next time. I really need to finish this paper."

Miller sighed and released Shay. "I guess I should be proud you're getting more studious." He reached for a hug, and Jo tried to shrink away, but he wasn't having it. He pulled her to his chest and rested his chin on the top of her head, his arms so tight around her, she could barely move.

"I'm all sweaty," she complained. "*You're* all sweaty."

"Then that means I did my job right." He released her, grinning. "All right, go on. Write the paper of your life."

Shay quickly hid her scowl when Miller turned to face

her again, her face transforming into a radiant smile. "You ready?"

Jo glanced around, realizing everyone else had trickled out.

"See you around, Palmer," said Miller. He raised his guard and lightly punched her shoulder, winked, then he and Shay turned and headed out. Jo hesitated long after she heard the door shut, listening to the buzz of the fan in the corner and staring at her reflection in the mirror. Her cheeks were still flushed and her sweaty hair was matted to the sides of her face. The room seemed larger now without anyone else in it.

"Hey."

Jo jumped at a knock on the door. A girl with dark brown braids poked her head inside. "Uh, are you all done in here?" She held up a lime green yoga mat. "Our class is supposed to start, but we're not supposed to go in until everyone from the last class is out."

"Oh." Jo hurriedly collected the rest of her things and headed for the door. "Yeah, sorry." She kept her head down as she shuffled past the other yoga attendees in the hall and slipped outside to walk back to her dorm, alone, as she'd done every night that week.

It was a clear night, the moon on full display overhead, the air chilly against her still-sweaty skin. She'd already finished her homework in the library earlier today, so a Netflix-in-bed night it was. Considering what she'd just put her body through, that was probably all she could manage right now anyway.

When she stepped into the suite, the common area

was full of boxes and plastic bins. So much so that Jo had to flatten herself against the wall and shuffle sideways just to get inside. Rap music pulsed from behind Addie and Liv's closed door, but the one to her room was wide open. Kayleigh was pacing back and forth inside, her hair tied up with a bright red bandana and her arms full of clothes. Jo set her bag on the floor and paused in the doorway.

"What's going on?"

Kayleigh jumped and brought a hand to her chest. "Holy hell. You scared me." She tossed her armful of clothes onto her bed, which had been stripped down to the bare mattress. "I hadn't expected you to be back yet."

Jo glanced around their room, her stomach tightening at the sight of each new fully-packed box. "What's going on?" she repeated.

"Well." Kayleigh sighed and propped her hands on her hips. "I'm moving out."

"I—what?"

"I applied for a new room weeks ago, and one just opened up across campus, so I'm gonna start moving my things in there tonight. I'll come back and get the rest tomorrow."

"Kayleigh." Jo stepped all the way into the room, forcing Kayleigh to actually meet her eyes. "Why? What's going on?"

Kayleigh sighed again. "Look, let's not make this weird, okay? It just wasn't working out for me. I'm sorry. But I think this will be what's best for both of us." She hoisted a box into her arms and slipped back out into the common area. "Like I said, I'll come back for the rest of my stuff tomorrow."

Jo opened her mouth again—to say what, she wasn't sure. Anything to keep Kayleigh from leaving. But she supposed there really wasn't anything you could say if someone didn't want to stay.

❧ 22 ❦

SENIOR YEAR - MARCH

JO FINISHED WITH THE LAST OF GRACIE'S HAIR AND DID A quick coat of hairspray. She'd ordered an Uber for her a while ago, and judging by the map on her phone, the car would be here any minute.

"There." Jo stepped back to admire her handiwork. The blonde curls spilled gracefully over Gracie's shoulders, the front sections twisted back and pinned to the crown of her head. They'd decided on a dainty gold chain around her neck and no earrings, since the dress spoke for itself. Its metallic finish caught the light every time Gracie moved, glittering and glowing like the light was coming from within.

Gracie stared back at her with wide, terrified eyes.

"Gracie." Jo clapped her on the shoulders. "You look hot, and it'll be fun. Miller will take good care of you, I promise. He's the best date ever."

Gracie nodded a few too many times.

Jo squeezed her shoulders and nodded toward the door. "Now go. Your car will be downstairs in, like, sixty seconds."

Gracie bit her lip, her hands wrapping around the tiny black clutch Jo had dug out from the back of her closet. "You're sure you'll be okay here?"

"Yes. Now *go*." Jo waved her off, and with one final glance in her direction, Gracie headed into the hallway and closed the door behind her.

At first, the silence was startling. The previous hour had been so full of chatter and activity, she'd been too busy and distracted to think about anything else. But now Gracie was gone, and Jo watched through the window as she climbed into the Uber, and the car sped off down the road.

Now it was just her. She'd probably get hell from Miller later on, but for now, she had the night to herself. She hadn't had much downtime the past few weeks. Maybe a quiet night was exactly what she needed. She could rent a movie and have a glass of wine. Order dinner in. Hell, she could break out the face masks and paint her toenails. Cautiously, she wove her way through the maze of makeup and hair products still littering the carpet and paused in the center of the room, her gaze lingering on a discarded pair of gold hoops sitting on the dresser.

The first Christmas present Miller had given her.

She shook her head and headed to the bathroom to collect everything she needed for the night. Arms full of face masks and nail polish, she plopped herself on the bed to scroll through the TV for a movie. She'd finally settled on an old favorite when her phone buzzed against the blankets. Her heart sank at the sight of Miller's name, but she didn't open the text. It was too late now, and even if he was mad, he was too much of a gentleman to be anything but a good date to Gracie tonight. They'd have to talk eventually. But eventually could wait until tomorrow.

She headed to the kitchen and let out a long sigh as she opened the fridge and realized she was out of wine. She opened a few cabinets, checking for any kind of liquid companion for the night, but came up empty-handed.

Well, shit.

A glance out the window confirmed the rain she heard on the roof, but still, she slipped on some shoes, threw a raincoat over her sweats, and headed for the door. Tonight would not be complete without a glass of wine. There was a liquor store just around the corner, and at this point, she really didn't care who saw her looking like this. If it weren't raining, she'd probably just walk. Today, though, she ducked her head against the rain and hurried over to her Jeep.

The man behind the counter nodded at her as she stepped inside. A few frat guys lingered over by the beers, but other than that, the store was empty. Jo headed straight for the wine, picking up two boxes—one red, one white. She paused in the aisle and bent over to inspect a nearby bottle that caught her eye. There was something familiar about it, though it was way out of her price range, so she knew she'd never bought it for herself. It had a sticker next to it on the shelf, advertising that it was local.

She straightened again, the pieces clicking in her head.

It was the wine her parents had ordered at dinner the other night with Miller.

The dinner Miller had still gone to despite everything that had happened that day.

She looked down at the boxes of wine in her hands. She was being a coward. She was being a coward *and* a bad friend.

"Fuck," she muttered, set the boxes back on the shelf, and turned to leave. The sight of the person coming through the door froze her in place. The bell chimed overhead as the girl stepped into the shop, her blonde hair damp from the rain. She lifted her head and spotted Jo before Jo had the chance to react.

"Hey." Kayleigh walked toward her, her rain boots squeaking with each step. "I'm actually so glad I ran into you."

Jo stared at her, momentarily lost for words. Kayleigh had never been outwardly hostile toward her, but their interactions usually consisted of them avoiding eye contact, pretending they hadn't seen each other, and carrying about their business. Kayleigh was definitely looking at her now, eyes wide, teeth deep in her lower lip.

Jo shifted beneath the weight of her stare. "I—oh? Why?"

"I wanted to apologize," she said in a rush, the words practically tripping over each other. She dropped her gaze at the word *apologize*, her voice lowering as she added, "I feel *so* bad."

Jo blinked, really confused now. She'd stopped waiting for an apology from Kayleigh years ago, but whatever this was about—whatever was making Kayleigh so fidgety and flushed—it was something more than just freshman year. Jo cleared her throat. "For what?"

Kayleigh shifted her weight and glanced at the slushy machines in the back corner, her gaze sweeping the rest of the store before coming back around to Jo, as if searching for someone to help her. "I didn't mean to tell him...it just sort of came out. He was asking about you—and sometimes he just talks *so* much and asks *so many questions,* and I just wanted him to stop. I didn't even think. I'm sorry."

"Kayleigh, I have no idea what you're talking about."

She covered her face with her hands, her next words coming out muffled. "I accidentally told Jordan about freshman year...with Grey and everything. I really didn't mean to, I swear."

Jo stared at her, her entire body tensing at just the sound of his name. "*You're* the one who told Jordan."

Kayleigh nodded, hands still firmly pressed to her face.

Jo shook her head, trying to clear it. "I didn't even know that you..." she trailed off, her throat tightening too much to speak.

Kayleigh finally dropped her hands and fidgeted with the zipper on her jacket. "I saw the tests in the bathroom trash."

For a moment, neither of them spoke. Jo didn't feel anything at the revelation, not at first. The anger, however, came shortly after.

"You knew the whole time?" Jo shook her head. "And still you...?"

Kayleigh dropped her gaze to her feet.

"Wow." Jo barked out a bitter laugh. She wasn't even that surprised—maybe hearing about it from Jordan had taken all of the shock away. Or maybe she was just done letting this drama suck her back in and take over her life.

Because beyond the lingering string of betrayal and anger, stronger than anything else was the relief.

It wasn't Miller. She'd never really thought it was—she couldn't truly believe that. But still.

"I have to go." Jo edged around Kayleigh, pulling her hood back up as she reached the front door. The rain was coming down harder now as she hurried to her car, her entire body trembling with building adrenaline. The rain hammered on the car as she sped back toward her apartment, the colorful reflections of the streetlights against the damp roads blurring past her.

She looked at the clock, then at her reflection in the rearview mirror, debating whether it was worth trying to pull herself together. She didn't even have a dress anymore —Gracie was in the nicest one she had. But if she pulled up to the reception looking like this, they might not let her in.

She checked the time again as she pulled into the parking lot, but it was barely an hour after the banquet was supposed to start. Miller was always the type to make an appearance and leave early, but this had been important to him. She glanced up at the side of the building. The window for his apartment was dark. She still had time.

She had just turned to grab her bag from the passenger seat when someone knocked on her window. She jumped and turned to see Miller crouched beside her car, squinting against the rain. He was in nothing but his suit, and it looked like he'd been out there for a while. He was completely drenched, his hair dripping against his forehead, clothes suctioned to his body. He swiped at his face, clearing the water from his eyes, and motioned for her to roll the window down.

She threw the door open and stepped out. The rain was coming down so forcefully now, it was almost painful. It pounded against the cars around them, the sound of it filling the parking lot. "What the hell are you doing?"

"What the hell am *I* doing?" He paused for a second and looked back toward the apartment building, his shoulders falling. "Why didn't you tell me?" he asked, his voice barely audible.

"Look, I should've given you a heads-up. I'm sorry, but I was just about to—"

"I'm not talking about Gracie. I mean, why didn't you tell me you were freaking out about the other night?"

Jo met his eyes, the blood draining from her face. "I—I guess I just needed some time to think—"

"Why didn't you just tell me that?" He looked away and wiped the rain from his face. "You think I haven't been freaking out over here too? That I haven't been an absolute fucking wreck since the moment you left that morning?"

She stared at him, speechless.

"Fuck." He kicked at the puddle of water accumulating at his feet and turned away.

Panic accumulated in her chest like a tangible weight, growing and building until it pressed down on her lungs with so much pressure she could hardly breathe. Staring at his back—the thought of him walking away. Water ran down her face. Whether it was from the rain or she'd started crying, she wasn't sure. Everything inside of her had been an absolute tangled mess since that night, but maybe it had been like that for him too. And she'd just pushed him away. Pushed him away and left.

"Miller, I—"

"If you regretted it, you could've just told me that," he said, his back still to her.

"Miller, no. That's not it," she insisted, her voice coming out shaky and thin. "It's just—I—" She scrambled for the right words, a way to explain. "It's not that at all."

He whipped back around, and in two long, deliberate steps, he crossed the distance between them and pinned her against the side of her Jeep, his hands in her hair.

"I need you to tell me if you want this," he murmured. "Because I can't pretend that I don't anymore."

Their eyes met, and water dripped from his hair onto her cheeks. When she hesitated, he started to pull away. But then she reached up, grabbed the back of his head, and crushed her lips to his.

And for a moment, that's all there was. All of the panic and second-guessing and confusion—it all went away. He was the deepest inhalation after holding her breath for a moment too long, and she was desperate for it, starving for it. She opened her mouth to him and wrapped her arms around his neck, her body responding before her mind had a chance. His body closed in around her, blocking her from the rain.

She pulled back, just an inch, as something occurred to

her. She looked up at him through wet lashes, her teeth starting to chatter. "Where's Gracie?"

"I took her home. She's the one who demanded I come and find you. Very...*passionate* friend you have there."

Jo couldn't picture Gracie standing up to Miller, or anyone for that matter. Apparently Jo's worries about being insensitive about Gracie's crush weren't warranted if she was playing full-on matchmaker.

Miller ran his hands up and down her arms as she hunched her shoulders against the cold.

"Can we go inside now?" he murmured. "And talk about this?"

She leaned into his chest, tucking her frozen fingers inside his suit jacket to shield them from the rain, and nodded.

JO'S ENTIRE BODY WAS SHIVERING FROM THE COLD BY THE time they made it back to her apartment, the rain completely soaked through her clothes and chilling her to the bone. Neither of them spoke as they headed up the elevator, and Miller followed her quietly to the bedroom. He sank onto the bench beside her bed, pulling off his drenched suit jacket as she slipped into the bathroom and cranked the shower to the hottest setting. She was about to strip off her wet clothes and attempt to thaw out her body when she paused and poked her head back out the door.

Miller glanced up at her from where he sat, his hands

firmly pressed together in his lap, his eyebrows drawn together in a harsh line.

Slowly, she raised her arm, extending her hand to him. He stared at it, the tension in his body ebbing away as he rose to his feet and stepped toward her, fingers tentatively sliding between hers. Steam filled the bathroom as she led him inside.

"I don't know how to do this," she admitted.

"I don't either," he said quietly, but he didn't let go of her hand. "But I want to try to figure it out."

She dropped her gaze and licked her lips, trying to find the right words, trying to make enough sense of it in her own head to explain. "I'm sorry that I freaked out—"

"I get it, Jo. I do. But I'm..." He shook his head and pressed his lips together, like he was arguing with himself over his next words. "I'm not him," he said quietly. "And I'm not going anywhere. Even if this doesn't work out, I'm not going anywhere."

She met his eyes, her throat thick. "I know." She reached up, fingers surprisingly steady as she started to undo the buttons of his shirt. His chest rose and fell with his breath as she reached the bottom and slowly slid the shirt off his shoulders.

"Jo," he breathed, and then he was kissing her, his hands in her hair, her back pressed against the sink. He pulled back just enough to pull the wet sweatshirt over her head and kick off his shoes. As her sweats and his dress pants joined the growing pile on the floor, she pressed a hand to his chest, pulling away just an inch.

"Just tell me this isn't going to ruin everything," she whispered. "Tell me this isn't a bad idea."

He brought both hands to the sides of her face and tilted her head up to look at him. "It isn't."

She didn't know how he could be so sure, but the certainty in his voice, the openness in his eyes, it was enough to make the panicking voices in her head quiet. It was enough to make her lift onto her toes and bring her mouth back to his. It was enough to make her let herself want this. He tightened his arms around her waist, lifting her feet off the ground and carrying her under the spray of the shower, letting the steam close in around them.

❧ 23 ❧

FRESHMAN YEAR - FEBRUARY

THE CLOCK TICKED STEADILY ON THE WALL. JO STARED AT the smallest hand as it worked its way around a full circle, then another. Dr. Radden's pen tapped on her notebook, perfectly in sync with each second. After the second hand had made three full circles, Dr. Radden cleared her throat, and Jo's gaze fell back to her face. She was younger than Jo had expected before entering her office, though her experience with therapists was limited to what she'd seen in bad movies. Dr. Radden looked thirty, max, with a blunt bob haircut and square glasses. She had soft, kind features, and wide eyes that made her look like she was genuinely interested in whatever you had to say. Or maybe she was. Maybe she was much more patient than Jo was. Even after sitting in complete silence for several minutes, she just sat there and waited.

Her office was cute. Welcoming, even. She had a blue couch and two cream-colored chairs in a sort of triangle formation. Jo had vaguely wondered as she'd sunk into the couch if it was some kind of psychological test. *What does your seating choice say about you?*

All of the artwork on the walls depicted beaches and sunsets. Her office was on the top floor of the building, and she had the curtains thrown back, exposing her view of the campus.

"We don't have to talk about anything you don't want to talk about today, Jo," she finally said.

Jo nodded, casting her gaze to her hands in her lap. She hadn't wanted to come here. Hadn't even realized she'd decided to until the appointment was already made, and now here she was. It had been a couple of months since the Winter Ball. Since running into Grey. Since Miller had started dating Shay and slowly been more and more absent in her life. Since her roommate decided she was too much to deal with.

She supposed one appointment here really couldn't make things any worse.

Not that she'd really had a choice. Her advisor said an appointment was mandatory if she didn't want to end up on academic probation with the way her grades were shaping up this year.

"Why don't you tell me a little more about your interests and what you do here on campus?"

Jo's shoulders relaxed a bit. That was an easy enough question. "I'm a photography major," she told her. "I had my own business back home in high school, so I'm trying to get that started up again over here. I'm in the photography club and doing photography for the school newspaper."

"Well, that's great. It seems you know exactly what you want to do."

Jo nodded. "It's always been the same for me."

"And is that what most of your friends do?" she asked. "Have you met them all through photography?"

Jo paused, the word *friends* getting stuck in her head. The first person who came to mind was Mare, her best friend from childhood. But she was all the way at UC Davis. The second person was Miller, who seemed just as far away these days. There were the girls from the photography club who she'd partied with a few times, but they didn't do much together sober. Her relationship with Addie and Liv had gone from acquaintances to straight up avoiding each other now.

And Kayleigh had transferred rooms out of the blue a few weeks ago, not even bothering to tell Jo until the day she was moving out. Everyone had congratulated her on being one of the only freshmen with a single now, but all Jo could think about was all of that empty space. And why Kayleigh had hated living with her so much that she went out of her way to move. She probably had been a downer to be around lately, spending more time in bed, less time going out.

They hadn't spoken since Kayleigh came to get the last of her things.

Jo stared at her hands again. "I guess I'm kind of lacking in that department at the moment."

Something nudged her knee, and she looked up to see

Dr. Radden holding out a box of tissues. It wasn't until then that she even realized she was crying.

"I guess that might be part of the reason I'm here," she said quietly. "The year started off so well, and it feels like it's all kind of falling apart now. And everyone just went on without me, and now I don't know what to do."

Dr. Radden nodded sympathetically. "A lot of people find that the first friends they make their freshman year don't end up being the friends they stay with all through college. It's very normal. Can I give you some advice?"

Jo wiped her face with the tissue and laughed. "I'm all ears."

"It sounds like you might have all of your eggs in one basket. And it's great to know what you want to do. But why not open yourself up to some more opportunities? Try some new things—you'll meet different people that way, maybe even find something you like as much as photography. There's actually a brochure on the first floor, right by the door, with all of the clubs and their contact information. You should grab one on your way out. Or maybe consider adding on a minor that you're interested in."

Jo nodded, even though the very idea of adding something else to her plate or joining a new club was exhausting. "I guess I could look into that."

"Jo," Dr. Radden's voice softened. "I spoke with your advisor. She said you started this year as a very promising student—great grades, your professors said you were engaged in class." She paused and leaned forward, her hands loosely knitted together in front of her. "Typically when we see academic performance change this drastically, there's an underlying cause."

Jo met her gaze, her throat suddenly tight, and mortifyingly, the backs of her eyes started to burn with the threat of tears.

"If you tell me what's going on, we can work with you."

Jo dropped her eyes and dug her nails into her palms to center herself. She didn't think she could force her mouth to form the words even if she wanted to. And where would she even start? It was all so overwhelming—this tangled mess of moments and pain. It was almost as if it had short-circuited her brain and caused some kind of memory loss, leaving her with no way to describe what had happened. Not coherently, at least. And a part of her didn't want to untangle the web. Just wanted to leave it shoved back into the darkest corner of her mind for as long as it would stay there.

And even if she managed to talk about it, she had a sinking feeling that Dr. Radden would get it all wrong. Even if her face didn't twist with judgement, she would make assumptions. That this was all from guilt or regret. And maybe that was the biggest problem—the guilt that comes from not feeling guilty at all.

"I understand if you don't feel comfortable enough to talk about it this time," Dr. Radden added after a while. "It's something we can build up to. This isn't a sprint, Jo. This can just be the first step."

Jo glanced up at the clock, startled to see their time was already up.

"I hope you'll come back to see me again," Dr. Radden

added. "You can always call the receptionist to make an appointment, or we just started an online portal where you can schedule things that way, if it's easier."

Jo nodded again, thanked her on her way out, and grabbed the brochure she'd mentioned before she left. She thumbed through the pages as she headed back across the quad to grab some lunch. Admittedly, there were more clubs than she'd realized, though she wasn't completely convinced throwing another into her schedule was going to solve any of her problems. The minor though. That wasn't a half-bad idea. All those extra classes would help keep her busy, at least.

"Jo, wait up!" Miller jogged up beside her, and she quickly dropped her hand holding the brochure so he couldn't see.

"Hi, stranger," she said.

He laughed and pushed his hair out of his face. "Yeah, I know things have just been really busy lately. Were you just seeing Dr. Radden?" He jabbed his thumb at the building behind them.

She ducked her head a little. "Yeah, actually. Guess I decided to take your advice after all."

He smiled. "I think that's great, Jo. How are you doing?"

She gripped the straps of her backpack and stared straight ahead. "Hanging in there."

Miller licked his lips and swallowed hard. "Jo, I—"

"*There* you are!" Shay hurried over in a pretty floral sundress, her hair done up in a braid-crown. She immediately attached herself to Miller's side, throwing both of her arms around one of his. "Hi, Jo." Her eyes looked Jo up and down, the movement so fast, it was almost imperceptible. But not quite. "I...I thought you and *I* were getting lunch," she murmured to Miller, though it was still plenty loud enough for Jo to hear, and Jo suspected Shay wanted it that way.

Miller opened his mouth and looked at Jo, but Jo was already shaking her head and took a step away from them. "I was actually just heading to a meeting for the photography club anyway. I'll see you guys around."

"Okay! Bye!" Shay waved.

Jo turned and headed back toward the academic buildings, even though she'd really been heading back to her dorm. There was no photography club meeting until tomorrow, but she didn't want a pity lunch invite, and she didn't want Shay glaring at her across the table the entire time if she accepted. Eating alone in her dorm was still infinitely preferable.

Jo didn't dislike Shay. She was clearly really into Miller, and she seemed to make him happy enough. And she couldn't even blame Shay for not wanting to share him with another girl, no matter how platonic it was. It wasn't Shay's fault that Miller was her only friend left, and the rest of her life was falling apart.

She dialed her mom's number as she climbed the stairs to her dorm even though she knew it was a bad idea. Chances were she wouldn't pick up, and Jo didn't know which she was dreading more.

"Johanna!" her mom's voice belted through the phone, loud enough that Jo had to hold it away from her ear as she

wrestled with her keys to unlock her door. Her eyes immediately skirted away from Kayleigh's empty side of the
room, which she still hadn't brought herself to fill. Luckily,
it didn't look like Addie or Liv were home either. She
closed her door, shutting off the rest of the suite, just in
case.

"Hi, Mom."

"How's it going, sweetheart? Your father and I were just
talking about you. We're having this big party for our
anniversary this weekend, and now that you're away at
college, who's going to take our pictures?"

Jo snorted. "I'm sure plenty of people there will know
how to work an iPhone."

"You're still coming home for Easter, right? I want
those pictures to be good so I can frame them."

"That's all I am to you now, isn't it? Your own personal
photographer," Jo teased.

"Well, of course. That's the only reason your father and
I had you. It was an investment."

Jo laughed and dug around on her desk for something
to eat. All of her solo meals in here had put a serious dent
in her stash. Finally, she found some microwavable mac and
cheese tucked in the back corner.

"How's school?" her mom asked.

Jo hesitated, mac and cheese in hand. She could tell her
mom. Tell her everything. But she'd learned a long time
ago that her mom wasn't the place to go if you wanted
comfort. It wasn't her fault, not really. She probably didn't
even realize she was doing it. But somehow, no matter how
serious the conversation, her mom always managed to steer

it back to her. Her problems. Her day. Until suddenly Jo was giving *her* comfort instead of the other way around. And she really just didn't have the energy for it today.

"It's good. I've actually got to go—I have a photography meeting. Just wanted to call and say hi."

"I'm glad you did! Bye, honey!"

"Bye, Mom."

Jo hung up and set the phone on her desk, staring at its dark screen. The silence of the room crowded in on her ears. She set the unopened mac and cheese beside the phone, her appetite suddenly gone. A lot of things seemed to be gone lately.

24

SENIOR YEAR - MARCH

Jo woke to the feeling of fingertips on her cheek. She blinked her eyes open to see Miller brushing the hair out of her face. The smallest hint of morning light was peeking through the window behind him. Faint, red creases lined the side of his face from the pillow.

She smiled and reached up to rub the sleep from her eyes. "Hey," she murmured.

He smiled back. "Hey."

She wiggled forward a bit until their foreheads touched, and his hand came to rest at the back of her neck.

"You know," he murmured. "I didn't notice it the first time, but you kind of snore a little."

She jabbed him lightly in the ribs. "I do not!"

"Don't worry," he chuckled. "It's cute."

"Hm." She flopped onto her back, and he propped himself on a single elbow to look down at her.

"You're not freaking out this time, are you?" he asked quietly.

She reached up to brush the hair out of his eyes, noticing the small pattern of freckles along his cheekbone that she hadn't seen before, and shook her head. "Are you?"

"Not at all."

She pinched her lips together to keep the stupid smile at bay, but it broke out just the same. "Good."

He grinned back at her and rolled so he hovered over her. "Good."

"Mill," she complained, a little breathless, as he leaned down to cover her mouth with his. The least he could do was let her brush her teeth first. But as his hand tightened around the back of her head, holding her firmly against him as his tongue swept into her mouth, suddenly, she didn't care anymore. Her hands slid up the sides of his ribs to find the hard planes of his back as he braced his hands on either side of her head. Her eyes fluttered shut as his lips trailed from her jaw to her collarbone.

"We can't just stay in bed all day," she murmured.

"Well, damn. That's exactly what I was intending to do." He pulled back just enough to look at her.

She slid her hands up to rest behind his head, a small smirk teasing at her lips. "Last night was really good."

"Glad you appreciated that." He leaned back down to brush a kiss right below her ear. "I thought it was some of my best work."

Laughing, she tugged on his arm until he flipped on her back beside her, his breathing coming out a little uneven. They lay there like that for a while, just staring at the ceiling, until he reached over, threaded his fingers through hers, and brought their hands to rest against his chest.

"What are you thinking about?" he murmured.

She kept her gaze trained on the ceiling even though she could feel him looking at her now. "The day you took me to the doctor," she admitted.

His body tensed, his fingers tightening slightly around hers.

"No, not like that. Not—in a bad way." She sighed. "I don't know. I just spent a long time not letting myself even think about that day."

"I know we haven't really talked about it, and I'm sorry if I ever made you feel like you couldn't," he said quietly. "I just never wanted to push you on it."

"No, I know. I didn't really want to talk about it for a while. It wasn't just you. I just—I felt like there was a way I was supposed to feel about it. And it just...wasn't...I don't know."

"Jo, however you feel about it is however you feel about it."

She turned her head to look at him, and he stared back with wide eyes, his eyebrows pulled together in concern. "Even now," she whispered. "I look back on it, and I'm just relieved." Her voice broke around the last word, and she pulled in a shaky breath. "Is that horrible?"

"God, no." He pulled her against him and rested his chin on the top of her head. "It's not horrible, Jo."

She let out another shaky breath, and his arms tightened around her. She cocooned herself in the warmth of his body, burying her head against his chest and breathing him in. "The point was—I just—" She sighed again. "Thank you. I don't think I've ever said that. But I don't know what I would've done if you hadn't been there."

He ran his fingers through her hair, pushing it back just enough to brush his lips against her temple. "I'm sorry you had to go through any of that at all," he said quietly.

She nudged him onto his back so she could prop her arms on his chest and look down at him. A slow smile spread over her face.

His returning smile was automatic. "What?" he asked.

"I don't know." She pressed her chin into her arms. "I guess it all just doesn't feel as...heavy anymore."

His smile faded, replaced by an expression she didn't understand. He reached up, his hand cupping the side of her face, and pulled her down until their mouths connected. But instead of the swift brush of lips she was expecting, he kissed her slow, deep. The kind of kiss she could melt into until it made her forget about absolutely everything else.

He rolled them back over so he was straddling her hips and pinned her arms over her head. She lifted a single eyebrow as he bent down so their lips were just an inch apart. "Omelet or pancakes?"

She let out a small, surprised laugh. "Well, you already know how much I like your pancakes."

"Done." He pressed a quick kiss to her forehead and rolled off of her again.

She bit her lip, watching as he slid out from under the covers and pulled on his boxer shorts. The golden rays of sun peeking through the window danced off the muscles of his back as he moved toward the hall, running a hand through his messy hair. He paused in the doorway and leaned his head against the frame, taking in the sight of her on the bed. "Just...don't go anywhere this time, okay?"

She smiled as she nuzzled back into her pillow. "I won't."

🎍 25 🎍

FRESHMAN YEAR - MARCH

IT WAS THE FIRST DAY THE DIZZINESS HADN'T BEEN ALL-consuming. Jo had been on the antidepressants for a week, and up until now, the disorientation had been so great, she'd barely been able to stand. She'd taken the whole week off from classes, claiming it was the flu, while she waited for her body to adjust and the side effects to subside. Being gone for a week definitely wasn't going to do her tanking grades any favors, but right now, she just couldn't muster the energy to care. The doctor told her it would take time for her to feel any improvement, and even then, it could take experimenting with different medications and dosages before they found the right fit—something she was desperately trying not to get discouraged about, because at least this was a step in the right direction.

Miller had stopped by the first few days with soup, but Shay had been with him, so they hadn't stayed long. It was probably for the best, anyway. She hadn't really felt up to pretending.

It was another Friday night without plans—which was fine. She was starting to get used to it at this point. Lacy and Tracy from photography club had invited her to some frat party like old times, but even though Jo was back on her feet, the idea didn't hold the kind of appeal it once had. She'd been all set to have a self-care movie night in her dorm when she saw it.

She shouldn't have read it. That was her first mistake. The second she saw the headline on her phone, she should've just scrolled away.

But she hadn't been able to help herself.

Grey from United Fates finally reveals inspiration behind top hit 'Johanna.'

She threw up immediately after reading it, and it was like she was in that empty apartment all over again. She read the entire thing in his voice, which was apparently still fully intact in her mind. She was hoping it would've faded by now.

Of course he hadn't mentioned where she was at now. What had happened to her. The way he'd hung up the phone, so easily forgetting all about the one thing that hadn't let Jo rest for months. The one thing she could never *not* think about.

And of all things to get hung up on, she somehow still managed to be surprised that he hadn't bothered to give her a heads-up. They hadn't spoken since the Winter Ball, and seeing as he hadn't bothered to tell her about the song itself before it came out, she wasn't sure why she'd expected anything different for an article. But sometimes, things got blurry in her mind. There were two versions of Grey. The one who held her hand, helped her roommate pick out a dress, and fell asleep with his head in her lap while they watched movies. And then there was *this*. The man under the lights with his face plastered across all of the newspapers.

The one who wrote the horrible things in that song.

He must've been thinking those things about her all along. She knew that now. But in the weak moments, she liked to let herself pretend, just for a moment, that the first version hadn't been all lies.

It was late, after most of the dorm had already ventured out to their various plans, when she headed to the small area with plastic picnic tables behind the building. It was cold, but the night air felt good against her skin—sharp and demanding. It was almost enough to give her a break from her thoughts. She needed to get out of her room anyway, away from the pregame Addie and Liv were throwing in their suite that they'd apparently forgotten to invite her to, or at least tell her about. She'd stepped out of her room with no makeup on and no bra to find a sea of strangers all looking at her like she was intruding, *in her own room.*

She curled into the bench in her pajama pants and a T-shirt, tilting her neck back to look at the stars.

The funny thing was, she hadn't thought about Grey in weeks. She'd stopped listening to the radio all together months ago so that song couldn't pop up and unexpectedly ruin her day. But today, the article had popped up in her newsfeed like some sort of cruel, cosmic joke. That no matter how hard she tried to distance herself from it all, it always managed to catch back up.

Headlights cut across the courtyard, momentarily blinding her, as a car pulled up and idled beside the curb. They were probably a DD picking someone up for a party. She angled her head back toward the stars, watching as her breath puffed up in a small cloud around her.

The driver's side door opened, and the car let out a series of *dings*. Jo glanced back over as a figure cut across the headlights, heading straight toward her. It wasn't until he was on the opposite side of the table that she recognized him.

She quickly swiped at her cheeks for tears that managed to squeeze themselves out.

Miller slid into the seat across from her and braced his forearms on the table. He, too, was in only a T-shirt, and he hunched his shoulders against the cold as he looked off at the expanse of trees to their side. "Are you okay?" he asked.

She thought about lying, but it was pretty clear she was very much not okay. "No," she admitted, her voice thick. "But you should go back to your car."

"Well, obviously I'm not going to do that."

Jo sniffled and glanced back toward his car, which was still beeping from the open door. "I don't want you here."

He finally turned to look at her. "Why?"

She shrugged. "Because you're always coming to my rescue."

He dropped his arms from the table. "And that's—a bad thing?"

"Yes," she insisted. "Because I don't want you to think of me as someone who always needs to be rescued."

"You know I don't see you that way."

She stared at him for a second, the headlights from his car lighting him from behind. "I thought you had a date with Shay tonight."

Miller twisted his mouth to the side and folded his hands back on the table. "I broke up with Shay."

"What?" Jo demanded. "Why? When?"

"Today." He scratched beneath his chin, and a small shiver ran through him. "I should've done it sooner."

Jo shifted on her seat, not really sure what she was feeling. "I thought—you really liked her."

He nodded, acknowledging this. "I did. But she wasn't..." He cleared his throat. "She told me what she said to you. Jo, I didn't know. I never would've..." He glanced down at his hands. "I never wanted you to stop hanging around, and I feel sick knowing you thought I did." He swallowed hard and got up to slide onto the bench beside her. "Jo, you're my best friend," he said quietly.

Jo took in a shaky breath, her chest feeling like it might explode with relief, but also like she might burst into tears again. She closed her eyes and leaned against his shoulder. "I missed you."

He threw his arm over her shoulders. "Will you please get in the car now?" he asked. "It's fucking freezing out here. You know I just drove all over campus looking for you? And you were over *here*, of all places."

"At my dorm? What a shock."

A laugh rumbled deep in his chest, and he pushed her away lightly. "Come on." He hopped up and extended a hand toward her.

She eyed his hand, but didn't move.

"You'll like what you find in the car," he insisted.

She raised her eyebrows, her gaze flickering back over to where it waited beside the curb. "You brought me a present?"

"A bribe," he corrected. "Take the bribe, Jo."

She smelled it the moment she slid into the passenger seat. He pulled up two fast food bags and set them on the center console, the smell of salt and grease filling the car. She lifted a corner to peek inside.

"Fries. Predictable but not disappointing." She eagerly popped one in her mouth and fished around for the box of chicken nuggets at the bottom of the bag as he pulled the car into the last spot in the parking lot.

Miller ripped open a ketchup packet with his teeth and nodded toward the back seat. Jo followed his gaze and let out an audible gasp. The entire back seat was full of plastic bags from the nearby grocery store. She twisted herself around to dump one out, and sure enough, the entire thing was full of Swedish Fish.

"How many bags did you buy?" she demanded.

He grinned. "Every single one the store had."

She clutched the bags to her chest, smelling the artificial delicacies through the wrapping. "You hate Swedish Fish," she reminded him.

"They're apology fish."

"Apology fish," she mused as she ripped open one of the bags and mixed them in with her French fries. She shot a triumphant grin at the look of absolute disgust on his face as she squished a fish and a fry together and shoved them into her mouth. "I like groveling Miller. Is there more?"

"My fries and fish aren't enough for you?"

She shrugged and licked the salt off her fingers. "It'll do."

"Well, actually." He twisted around to reach into the back seat and appeared with his laptop in hand. "Have you seen the new *Ugly Dead?*"

Her eyes widened. "I didn't even know it was out."

He set the laptop up on the dashboard as the opening credits filled the screen. He twisted his head to look at her as she reclined her seat and readjusted the food in her lap.

"I may not have thought this out very well. We could go somewhere more comfortable, if you want."

"Miller."

He raised his eyebrows.

She smiled, leaned over to wrap her arms around one of his, and rested her head against his shoulder. "This is perfect."

SENIOR YEAR - MAY

JO WAS RUNNING LATE. IT WAS ENTIRELY MILLER'S FAULT, of course. She'd tried to go to bed at a reasonable time last night, but he'd always been able to operate on laughable amounts of sleep and didn't seem to understand the concept of needing rest. It had started out innocent enough, a scary movie and candy, as they usually did. They made it about halfway through the movie before Miller climbed on top of her, and then that was the end of that.

She rushed through her room, picking up different pieces of jewelry as she went, and paused to check her makeup in the mirror one last time. Her hair was down and curled today—the same way she'd styled it for her high school graduation, actually, though the white dress she'd found this year was much more flattering than that one had been. This one was off the shoulder and had a cut out in the center, a thin layer of lace on the top half. She readjusted her cords and sashes over her shoulders, making sure all five were visible.

"Jo!" Miller called from the kitchen. "If we don't leave now, we're not going to make it."

She quickly bent over and slipped on her heels, then grabbed her bag from the dresser and strode out of her room.

"What?" she asked calmly. "I'm ready."

He grinned and bent down to kiss her on the cheek. "You look beautiful, as always."

She straightened his tie and pushed the hair back that always seemed to be falling in his eyes. His shoulders were overflowing with all of his cords—fourteen of them, last time she counted. "Did you order an Uber? There won't be any parking," she reminded him.

He held up his phone where a mini car approached their building on the map.

"Meredith texted me," said Jo as they headed downstairs. "She got a seat with my parents. I can't wait for you to meet her."

Miller squeezed her hand. "And you get to meet *my* mom. Busy day."

"You're sure she's not going to think I'm some kind of *floozy* for moving in with you?"

He snorted at the word *floozy* and shrugged as they waited at the curb for the car to arrive. "My parents got married after knowing each other for five months, and they lived together for three of those. Why? You think your parents aren't going to like it?"

Jo crossed her arms over her chest, hunching her shoulders a bit against the breeze. Hopefully her seat wouldn't be in the shade today. "My mom would fully support us running off to Vegas and eloping today. My dad...well, we'll just make sure you're sitting next to my mom at lunch. Maybe throw Mare in there as a buffer."

He took her hand and kissed the back of her knuckles. "I'm not worried about it. Worse comes to worse, tell them we're just roommates because we both have internships in town."

She snorted. "Oh yeah. I'm sure that will be *real* believable."

"Jo."

She looked over at him. "What?"

He smiled softly. "I love you."

She rolled her eyes, but smiled back.

The car pulled up, vibrating with some country song. Miller opened the back door, but froze before climbing in.

Jo peeked around his shoulder to find two of the three seats in the back already taken, as well as the passenger seat in the front.

"Did you order a share?" she demanded under her breath.

"Shit." He glanced at his watch, then started climbing into the remaining seat.

"Miller!"

"Come on." He waved his hands at her. "We're going to be late. You can sit on my lap."

She scowled at him, but climbed in nonetheless, bunching up her robe in her hands. The other passengers were also all decked out in graduation attire, but Jo didn't recognize any of them. The car pulled away from the curb abruptly, and she braced herself against the seat.

Miller grabbed her hips to steady her. "I've got you," he murmured.

The déjà vu was momentarily staggering. She glanced at him over her shoulder, and he offered her a guilty smile. But she couldn't even muster a trace of her earlier annoyance. She reached up and pushed the dark waves of hair out of his eyes. His smile dimmed, a question rising to his eyes instead, but she turned back around before he could say anything.

A lump was rising to the back of her throat out of nowhere, and she had to clench her jaw to keep the burning in the backs of her eyes at bay. Maybe it was the flashbacks of the night they'd met freshman year in this exact position, or maybe it was something else.

She'd been so worried that crossing this line with him would ruin everything. And she was almost afraid of saying it out loud in case it jinxed them, but everything so far had been so...*easy*. Natural. And for the first time in a long time, she wasn't worried about much of anything at all. He made it so easy to believe that despite everything, somehow, someway, everything was going to be okay.

The car dropped them off at the edge of the parking lot just as the graduates started lining up. Miller grabbed her hand as they jogged across the lawn, holding on to their caps as they went.

Miller gave her a quick kiss on the cheek, then paused, holding her face between his hands. "I'll find you after, okay?"

She nodded and waved him on. He gave her one last smile before running ahead to find his spot in line while Jo fell into place along the other *P* last names.

"Johanna." The guy in front of her turned around and smirked, his shoulders nearly overflowing with chords.

"Oh my God, Felix, hi. Uh, congrats?"

He nodded. "Same to you."

Her phone dinged inside her robe. "Sorry, sorry," she muttered as she fished around for it—she wasn't technically supposed to have it on her, but the ceremony was going to be *hours* long. She glanced around to make sure no professors would yell at her before pulling it out.

Meredith: *You didn't tell me Miller was that hot. Also, you look cute.*

Jo looked up, scanning the crowd ahead. A hand shot out above the rest of the heads, then Meredith was straight up standing on her chair. Her blonde hair was tied up in a bun on the top of her head, her pretty pink dress rustling in the breeze. Tears immediately sprung to Jo's eyes at the sight of her, and she waved her arm over her head. Meredith blew her a kiss before jumping back down into her chair. Her parents stood too, waving and grinning—her mom even had a life-size poster with her face printed on it.

A second wave of déjà vu crashed into her as she thought about four years ago as she walked across the stage with her best friend. Somehow, it simultaneously felt like yesterday and a lifetime ago. The past four years were a bit of a blur, but also, so much had happened. And all she really knew was, as she stood there and prepared to cross a stage for the second time, she felt different than she did before. There was probably a word for it that she didn't know—Miller was always the one who had a way with words, not her—but it felt something like hope. That somehow, through the tears and the late nights and the disasters during her time here, she'd come out like this. She'd come out feeling much more like herself than she had in a long time. Maybe more than she ever had before.

Jo laughed as her mom pumped the cardboard version of her face up and down, and her father put two fingers in his mouth and let out a long whistle. There'd been a lot of things they hadn't been there for, and she'd spent a long time convincing herself that she didn't care about that. But they were here now. They were here today. And it wasn't enough to erase the other times, but maybe it was a start.

She quickly rubbed the tears away before they had the chance to ruin her makeup, blew out a calming breath, and faced forward again as the orchestra music started to play.

Thank you for reading! Reviews are one of the best ways to support authors. If you enjoyed this book, please consider leaving a review on the site where you got it!

See where it all started in The Anti-Virginity Pact...

Preachers' daughters aren't supposed to be atheists.

They're also not supposed to make pacts to lose their virginity by the end of the year, but high school senior Meredith Beaumont is sick of letting other people tell her who to be.

Spending the last four years as Mute Mare, the girl so shy just thinking about boys could trigger panic attacks, Meredith knows exactly what it's like to be invisible. But when a vindictive mean girl gets her manicured claws on the anti-virginity pact and spreads it around the school— with Mare's signature at the bottom—Mare's not so invisible anymore. She just wishes she was.

Now the girls mutter "slut" as they pass her in the hall, and the boys are lined up to help complete her checklist. When she meets a guy who knows nothing of the pact, their budding romance quickly transforms from a way to get her first time over with to a genuine connection. But when the pact threatens to destroy her new relationship and the fragile foundation of her seemingly perfect family, Mare has to decide what's more important: fixing her reputation and pleasing her parents, or standing up for the person she wants to be.

The Anti-Virginity Pact is a coming of age young adult novel that acts as a companion to The Anti-Relationship Year. Available now!

SIGN UP FOR MY AUTHOR NEWSLETTER

Sign up for Katie Wismer's newsletter to receive exclusive content and be the first to learn about new releases, book sales, events, and other news!

www.katiewismer.com

ABOUT THE AUTHOR

Katie Wismer is a die-hard pig lover, semi-obsessive gym rat, and longtime sucker for a well-written book. She studied creative writing and sociology at Roanoke College and now works as a freelance editor in Colorado with her cats Max and Dean.

When she's not writing, reading, or wrangling the cats, you can find her on her YouTube channel Katesbookdate.

You can sign up for her newsletter at katiewismer.com, or check out her instructional videos on writing and publishing on Patreon.

patreon.com/katiewismer

instagram.com/katesbookdate

goodreads.com/katesbookdate

bookbub.com/authors/katie-wismer

facebook.com/authorkatiewismer

amazon.com/author/katiewismer

twitter.com/katesbookdate

Made in the USA
Middletown, DE
03 April 2021

36829492R00175